HOBGOBLIN

and the
SEVEN STINKERS
of RANCIDIA

Hazy Fables Book #1

Till Ellie och Astrid.
– K.S.

ISBN: 978-1-948931-04-5

First edition: September 2019
Published by Hazy Dell Press, LLC

Printed in China.

10 9 8 7 6 5 4 3 2 1

Find all Hazy Dell Press books at hazydellpress.com.

HOBGOBLIN

and the
SEVEN STINKERS
of RANCIDIA

By Kyle Sullivan

Illustrated by Derek Sullivan

HAZY DELL PRESS
PORTLAND · SEATTLE

Table of Contents

FIDDLEFART RAISES A STINK

Once upon a time in the stinky land of Rancidia, it was very good to smell bad and very bad to smell good. Everyone smelled awful, but that's the way they liked it.

Rancidians took great pride in their personal flavors of stink. But their deepest pride came from the sick symphony of funk they created when their odors blended together.

This pungent country was divided into seven

uniquely smelly districts: Tooterville, Pootonia, Morassia, Methania, Lousyana, Fungalo, and Cryptonia. Each district elected an official to represent its citizens at Rancidia's capital building—the Onion Palace above downtown Tooterville.

These elected officials, known as the Seven Stinkers of Rancidia, worked hard to ensure all Rancidians enjoyed equality and stinking freedom, regardless of their particular scent.

But that was once upon a time, before a horrible ogre named Fiddlefart stormed the Onion Palace, kicked out the Seven Stinkers, and took over Rancidia. Just like that, a healthy democracy became a wicked kingdom.

And while democracies are supposed to celebrate everyone, wicked kingdoms celebrate only one: the person in charge. In Rancidia, Fiddlefart was in charge. So, naturally, his first order of business was to give himself the made-up title of Grossest Smelling in the Land. He had a trophy made and everything.

Fiddlefart protected this made-up title with a passion that was all too real. Whenever the ogre caught a whiff of competition, he would wipe it out by ordering a scrubbing, which was by far his

favorite punishment.

That's right: Fiddlefart would disgrace his poor, smelly enemies with a bath. The thought of it alone was enough to send a shiver down any Rancidian spine.

The ogre king's next move was to make sure only he received the spotlight—or, for that matter, any light at all. He cut Rancidians off from sulfide gas, their only power source. Rancidians adored this potent, yellow gas, and not only because it smelled like rotten eggs. Without it, they struggled to keep their homes warm, brightly lit, and at maximum stink.

For many years, Fiddlefart's cruelty left everyone feeling gasless and miserable. They all longed for the days when they lived free and together as a musky medley of diverse and disgusting smells.

So, Rancidians began to whisper. They exchanged secret plans and rebellious words. They met quietly in the shadows where the king could not see or hear—or smell. In their darkest moment, Rancidians could sniff a faint scent of hope.

But whispers weren't enough. They needed a hero, or perhaps a handful of heroes, to help the hopeful scent blossom into a full-on stench of freedom.

And heroes do have a way of emerging in even the stinkiest situations. In fact, at this very moment, one such hero is dozing in the muck on a bean farm in the Unincorporated Mucklands.

He maybe doesn't look like a hero, and he definitely doesn't know he's a hero. But to stinky creatures every-where, he smells exactly as a hero should: dreadful.

While some heroes wear capes or glittery spandex, and others carry magic wands or sport bulging muscles, some heroes don't fit into pre-existing molds. Some heroes emerge unexpectedly to solve unexpected problems.

Some heroes aren't really that brave, nor all that smart. Some heroes are hobgoblins who smell like a fart.

CHAPTER 1

THE SCRUBBING ORDER

"**H**obgoblin!?" bellowed King Fiddlefart. "The *bean* farmer!?"

A trio of startled stinkbirds flapped away from the Onion Palace's chamber window and into the moonlit sky. The ogre king, in his black mold vest and corpse flower crown, leaned out of the window. He scowled down at the dark, gloomy buildings of downtown Tooterville.

Bright light and sulfide gas swirled into the night around the edges of the ogre's enormous body. He was quite upset, but he gained a small measure of joy by sneering at the dim and sorrowful community beneath him.

With a dismissive snort, he twirled away from the window and stomped across his chamber like a gigantic mutant toddler.

Piles of rotten garbage and spoiled food cluttered the chamber's every surface. Mold and decaying matter burst out of every shelf, drawer, nook, and cranny. Several pipes released thin wisps of sulfide gas that drifted around the mounds of filth. The dried corpses of piranhas, tarantulas, lizards, and bats were strung together and draped across the walls and ceiling.

Fiddlefart grabbed a handful of dripping purple fungus off a table and rubbed it feverishly on his face and under his arms.

"This can't be right! He's just a farmer in the Unincorporated Mucklands! He's not even a Rancidian citizen! And I'm the KING OF RANCIDIA!" he screamed. "I *must* smell grosser than him! My self-image depends on it!"

From a platform jutting out from a hole in the wall, the Burping Bullfrog watched without expression. He was old and withered, with a frail white beard and warts covering his body. "I can smell anything and everything at once," he croaked. "My psychic belches do not lie."

"Fine. Just belch again!" cried the ogre. With a pouty grunt, he slumped into his throne (which was really just a heaping pile of garbage). "Maybe you belched a mistake. Or…maybe it was indigestion or something!"

"As you wish." The frog was losing interest. As

a magic all-smelling frog who had lived for many centuries, the Burping Bullfrog had served dozens of masters. He ranked Fiddlefart as the worst of them by a wide margin. "But you have to ask using the official words."

Fiddlefart rolled his eyes. "Fine," he said. "Whatever."

The ogre took three giant steps across the room and stood facing the bullfrog. Phlegm rattled around as he cleared his throat. With arms crossed, he recited:

Burping Bullfrog in the wall,
who smells grossest of them all?

The Burping Bullfrog sat on his platform, motionless. He let the silence settle in around him. Then, suddenly, the frog grunted, and his eyes rolled back in his head. His nostrils sucked in the air around him, and he began to tremble.

His vacuum-like sniffing intensified as the trembling worsened into violent rumbling. The grunts grew louder and more frenzied. For a brief second, Fiddlefart considered hiding behind his garbage throne. But then, at once, the rumbling stopped.

After a moment of silence, a loud, dank, ghastly burp erupted from the bullfrog's mouth. The burp released green and purple vapors that swirled and twirled in front of his face. Then, the frog spoke:

Blurpity blorpy, blinkity bly,
Fiddlefart, you are one stinky guy.

"Go on…" said Fiddlefart with an impatient twirl of his finger.

The green and purple vapors began to form an image. The ogre king cocked his head to the side and squinted, but he couldn't make it out.

The bullfrog continued:

It's true your sick aroma
would wrench any nose,
but compared to Hobgoblin
you smell like a rose.

As the Burping Bullfrog croaked out these words, the burp vapors took shape. They formed into the beady eyes, long, curved nose, and dopey grin of the one and only Hobgoblin.

The vision of Hobgoblin blinked casually while six little flies buzzed around his oval head. Seemingly unaware he was being watched, the vapor-formed Hobgoblin farted and let out a little giggle. Then, in a magical swirl, the vision vanished.

"Impossible!" yelled the king, kicking a moldy pumpkin across the room. "There's no way! I don't believe it!"

Fiddlefart tugged at his ears, let out a chamber-rattling wail, and slashed the air around him with a series of unskilled karate chops.

Frantically, the king sniffed his left armpit and then his right. "Have I lost it?" he asked. "Am I losing my stinky edge?"

You've been losing your stink now
for quite a long while,
but the farmer's aroma
grows more and more vile.

"You weren't supposed to answer that!" screamed the ogre king as angry tears burned his eyeballs.

He clenched his eyes shut to fight away the tears. Taking a deep breath, the ogre king attempted to relax by repeating what he called his "smell-empowerment mantra":

"I smell worse than garbage, I smell like the sewer, I smell worse than garbage, I smell like the sewer…"

Taking this as his cue to leave, the Burping Bullfrog gave a bow, backed into his hole in the wall, and silently closed his little door.

The mantra had worked: Fiddlefart calmed down enough to take action. Or at least enough to order someone else to take action.

He trampled through garbage to the chamber door, opened it halfway, and screamed through the crack: "Huntress!!"

Promptly, as if she had been lurking only feet from the door, a squirrel wearing a hooded cloak and a wooden mask entered the chamber. She had a bushy chestnut tail and smelled of cinnamon. She came armed with a crossbow, a scrub brush, and a steely expression.

She stood there quietly as Fiddlefart, with his back to the squirrel, sprayed himself with an aerosol can labeled SHARK FARTS.

"Yes, Your Disgustingness," she said, her watchful eyes aimed at the king.

Fiddlefart jumped in surprise. He scrambled to hide the can of shark fart spray in a pile of garbage. The Huntress silently scoffed—it was an open secret throughout the kingdom that Fiddlefart artificially enhanced his nasty odor.

The ogre cleared his throat, walked over to the window, and pretended to look thoughtfully down at Tooterville.

Without turning around, he said: "There's a hobgoblin bean farmer in the Mucklands in need of a scrubbing, and you're just the woman for the job. You're my most trusted minion, but I don't really trust anyone. You'll have to prove to me you've scrubbed the hobgoblin…"

The ogre whirled around theatrically. He was holding a glass jar.

"…by bringing back his flies in this!"

The Huntress took the jar in both of her paws.

Fiddlefart continued. "As everyone knows from fables and nursery rhymes, a hobgoblin's flies would never leave their hobgoblin on purpose. They live for the creature's farty stench. However!"—Fiddlefart gestured to the scrub brush on her belt—"If you scrubbed him so badly that he lost his farty stench, the flies would no longer recognize him. Their little fly brains would be jumbled. They'd be sad, confused, and so very easy to capture."

The ogre grinned at his own devilishness. The Huntress looked Fiddlefart in his bloodshot eyes and said, "As you wish, Your Stinkiness."

Silently, she slipped out the door.

Alone once again, King Fiddlefart returned to his window, resumed his mantra, and filled the chamber with an unhappy fart.

CHAPTER 2

THE BEAN FARMER

"Prrummpf! Pruumpf! Paarruuumpf!!"

Soulful toots rumbled across the neat, steamy rows of bean plants. Taking a break from tooting, Hobgoblin propped his foot up on the short, rickety fence that surrounded his mud hut. He watched the sun melt into the horizon as sweat trickled down his loaf-shaped forehead.

It was the end of another hard workday on the bean farm. Hobgoblin, with kind, buttony eyes and a green cloud of stench billowing around him, was saluting the occasion as he always did: by tooting his heart out on a rusty tuba. It was a cherished family heirloom that went back many generations.

Six flies buzzed in lazy figure eights above Hobgoblin's head as he gazed across the Unincorporated Mucklands. Hundreds of bean plants dotted the landscape of mulchy sludge. To his right, large, smelly trees marked the beginning of the Fetid Forest.

The famously stinky hobgoblins had farmed this land for centuries. As he was the last of his kind, Hobgoblin was just called Hobgoblin. It had been a very long time since there was another hobgoblin around, and he couldn't remember what they had called him, if anything. He was very forgetful.

"Prumpf! Pruumpf! Prmpf! Prmpf! Prmpf!!"

Hobgoblin resumed his toots. The six flies took turns riding the current of hot air that burst out of the tuba with every "prumpf."

The flies were Hobgoblin's constant companions, and really, his only companions. The one exception was a monthly visit from a cranky warthog from Pootonia. On the sixth day of every month, the gnarled beast plodded through the Mucklands with his squeaky wheelbarrow to deliver supplies and haul away harvested beans.

Much to Hobgoblin's discomfort, the warthog would also deliver disturbing updates about neighboring Rancidia and its ogre problem. These updates distressed Hobgoblin immensely, so he had spent the last several years trying his best to ignore them. He'd much rather focus on pleasant things like tooting— both on his tuba and otherwise.

The flies continued riding the tuba current, every new toot an opportunity to practice flips and twists and twirls. Thanks to these flies, Hobgoblin was never, ever lonely. He loved them very much, and they loved him. The special bond that developed between hobgoblins and their flies was well known across Rancidia and its neighboring lands. In fact, there was an old Rancidian saying for best friends: "They're just like flies on a hobgoblin."

Once again, the tooting stopped. The flies paused their buzzing and toot riding to follow Hobgoblin's eyes southward. He was looking far into the distance, past the districts of Cryptonia and Pootonia, all the way to the Onion Palace that loomed over the land. The sunset bathed the palace in a soft lavender light.

Arranging themselves into a single-file line, the flies glided onto Hobgoblin's head and took a seat. They looked out toward the Onion Palace and let out six tiny, high-pitched sighs.

The flies felt bad for the Rancidians, and they loathed the ogre king. They stayed informed on what was happening in Rancidia thanks to a group of gadflies who accompanied the warthog every month. The gadflies warned that the ogre was scrubbing stinky creatures by the day, and Hobgoblin could easily be next. It's true that gadflies loved to gossip, but this seemed very real, and very scary.

Again, the flies sighed in unison.

"I know what you're thinking, guys," said Hobgoblin with his own sigh. "The Onion Palace makes you think of onion soup, and you wish we could eat some for dinner. I'm sorry, but all we have to eat is bean curdle."

The flies gave each other worried glances. Hobgoblin didn't seem to fully understand the danger he was in, but the flies sure did. They couldn't bear to think of their beloved friend without his stink. A hobgoblin without stink would be like a bird without wings.

On the rare occasions when Hobgoblin showed the tiniest amount of concern about the ogre king, it was always short-lived. He was very easily distracted.

"Turd blossoms!" yelled Hobgoblin.

The shocked flies instinctively darted into the little tufts of hair by Hobgoblin's ears for protection. They peeked out to see him pointing to the Fetid Forest's tree line, where little pink flowers sprang from the muck.

Rare and delicious turd blossoms were one of Hobgoblin's favorite snacks. The sight of them excited him so much that he forgot two very important things: 1) he was holding a tuba, and 2) he was standing behind a fence.

Lurching forward with his eyes on the turd

blossoms, Hobgoblin dropped the tuba, tripped on it, tumbled over the short fence, and splattered into the muck. Panicked, the flies scattered into the air.

Sitting on his butt in the muck, Hobgoblin tried to figure out how he got there. Then something in the forest caught his eye. Returning to Hobgoblin's head, the flies saw it, too—it was almost as if a shadow had slipped behind a tree.

Hobgoblin's heart raced and he sniffed the air. He was concerned he might pick up the scent of something scary, like a troll or a forest hyena or a perfumist.

Sure enough, Hobgoblin picked up a scent, but it wasn't anything he'd ever smelled before. It was strong and mysterious, with a slight trace of cinnamon.

Hobgoblin shivered. There was a weird smell creeping through the air, and for once he wasn't to blame.

The flies also smelled it. They knew Hobgoblin could be skittish at times, but in this case, they understood his fear. They didn't know what lurked in the forest. But they knew it smelled unfamiliar. It smelled disturbing. It smelled like danger.

"Hmm," said Hobgoblin. "On second thought,

those turd blossoms don't look ready to pick quite yet."

With a wary glance to the tree line and with his flies nervously gripping his hair, Hobgoblin picked himself up from the muck, gathered his tuba, hopped back over the fence, and went inside.

He closed the door and peered out of a side window into the darkening woods. Whatever it was had vanished. Although he tried to ignore it, somewhere deep down Hobgoblin knew this wasn't a troll or a forest hyena or a perfumist—this was something much worse. From that same deep-down place, Hobgoblin got the feeling this had something to do with the situation in Rancidia.

As Hobgoblin watched the forest through his window, a disturbing vision flashed through his mind. He imagined a huge, menacing ogre lurking in the shadowy depths of the forest. A shiver skittered across his neck. For the first time in a very long while, Hobgoblin wished his door had a lock.

Later that night, Hobgoblin got ready for bed by rubbing his face with mud and rinsing his mouth with sludge. Once he felt suitably soiled for sleep, he sat down on the soft mound of muck that he used for a bed. The flies sat on top of his head with their eyes closed and their hands clasped before them.

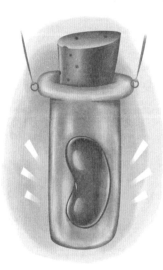

Candlelight gently danced across their faces. Hobgoblin grasped the corked vial he wore around his neck. Inside was a little normal-looking bean. He kissed the vial, closed his eyes, and interlaced his fingers. He then recited an ancient hobgoblin prayer.

"Dear Pre-Bean," he said.

"You're the first bean ever harvested by a hobgoblin in the Mucklands. You are the source of our pride, our livelihood, and our wonderful, hilarious farts. For that, we thank you."

The flies nodded in quiet agreement.

Eyes still closed, Hobgoblin let loose a respectful, ceremonial fart. The flies applauded in an adorable, barely audible sort of way.

Hobgoblin yawned, and the flies nestled onto his

pillow—a burlap sack stuffed with dried beans. He patted each of them on the head in turn and said, "Nighty night, little guys."

Before he lay down for the night, Hobgoblin walked across the room to the little nook in the wall where a candle faintly burned. He had once powered the electric lights of his mud hut with delightfully nasty-smelling sulfide gas, but the cranky warthog had stopped delivering it several years ago.

Hobgoblin didn't mind the candlelight so much, having recently overcome a fear of fire. But without sulfide, it was far chillier at night than it used to be. He missed the warm, stinky drafts of gas that used to waft through his hut all night.

He blew out the candle, and the darkness washed over them. Nestling into his muck bed, he covered himself with empty burlap bean sacks.

Hobgoblin smiled as he listened to the gentle breathing of the flies beside his head. The room settled with comfort, calm, and the familiar aroma of bedtime farts.

Minutes later, just as the first snore escaped Hobgoblin's nose, something slipped into the hut, silent but deadly. The something creeped into the bedroom, struck a match, and ignited a torch. The room blazed with flickering light.

The flies gasped, and Hobgoblin choked on his own saliva. As their eyes adjusted, a masked squirrel took shape, occupying their entire frame of vision. In one paw she held the fiery torch, in the other she held a scrub brush. It was aimed directly at Hobgoblin.

CHAPTER 3

THE OGRE'S ASSASSIN

Hobgoblin's scream was backed by six squeaky shrieks from his flies.

The squirrel poked the scrub brush into Hobgoblin's nose. "Do exactly as I say, Hobgoblin," she said. "Or I'll scrub you so hard, your flies won't recognize your scent."

Hobgoblin gulped. A shrill stress fart escaped under his burlap covers.

"Yes, ma'am," he said.

The flies nodded earnestly, ready for their orders.

"Get up," said the squirrel. "We're going into the Fetid Forest, where there are no witnesses. Dress appropriately."

Hobgoblin's tiny eyes darted nervously from the crossbow and arrow-filled quiver slung around the squirrel's shoulder to the pouch hanging on her back stuffed with who knows what cleaning products.

His eyes bulged a little when he noticed Fiddlefart's royal badge pinned to her cloak—a stinky, rotten corpse flower. He tried to gulp again, but his throat felt like a sock crammed with sawdust, so he ended up with a crooked frown.

The flies buzzed in nervous loops above Hobgoblin's sweat-soaked head. Without taking his eyes off the squirrel, Hobgoblin grabbed a cloak from his coat rack and, fingers trembling, fastened it around his neck.

The squirrel blew out her torch to steep the hut in darkness once again. Hobgoblin felt the scrub brush jab into his back.

"OK," said the squirrel in her raspy, no-nonsense voice. "Now, march."

Hobgoblin marched stiffly toward the door like a toy soldier.

"Hey, knock it off! You don't have to march like that," said the squirrel.

"Oh, sorry…" said Hobgoblin uncertainly. They left his mud hut and headed for the forest. Not sure how to march correctly, Hobgoblin took deep knee bends with his elbows fixed at right angles.

"Stop it!" said the squirrel, jabbing him in the back.

"I don't know how to march!" wailed Hobgoblin, afraid she was going to scrub him at any moment.

The squirrel stopped and let out an irritated groan. Gesturing with the scrub brush, she explained: "You don't have to *march* march. It's a figure of speech. Just walk normally into the forest and head northeast. I'll direct you where to go."

"Just walk normal," said Hobgoblin. "Got it."

After a few hesitant head bobs and practice steps, he remembered how to walk normally (at least normally for him) and headed for the green, blue, and purple trees of the Fetid Forest.

Under usual circumstances and during the day, Hobgoblin loved the Fetid Forest and its bounty of rotten, moldy, and sticky smells. However, his feelings were quite different at nighttime with a scary squirrel poking a scrub brush into his back.

The forest was completely dark and very noisy. Hobgoblin and his flies had no idea what was out there spattering the murky air with chirps, scratches, sniffs, coughs, and giggles—and they didn't care to find out. They flinched at every sound and winced every time the squirrel barked an order or jabbed Hobgoblin with the brush.

"Head to the right," said the squirrel.

"Yes, ma'am," said Hobgoblin.

"Don't call me 'ma'am,'" said the squirrel.

"OK, um, squirrel lady," said Hobgoblin.

"Don't ever call anyone 'squirrel lady,'" said the squirrel. "Just call me Huntress if you have to call me anything."

"OK, Huntress," said Hobgoblin. Something sneezed in the trees and Hobgoblin jumped in surprise.

"Keep going!" said the Huntress. "Don't worry about the things in the forest. I'm the only creature that brings you danger."

"Yes, Your Huntress," stammered Hobgoblin. "I mean, My Huntress. No! I mean, just Huntress." The flies smacked their foreheads in disbelief—if Hobgoblin was going to make it through this without getting scrubbed, he really needed to stop testing the squirrel's patience.

"Do you know where Fresh Falls is?" asked the Huntress.

Hobgoblin couldn't speak. The end point of the dreaded Rinsey River, Fresh Falls was a pure, clean, and glittery waterfall that emptied into the Pool of Purity. Everyone learned at a young age where it was—so they knew exactly where to avoid.

According to the folklore, once the glistening waters of the Rinsey River passed through Fresh Falls, they became infused with magical cleansing powers. The story went that if you dipped so much as a single toe into the Pool of Purity, you'd never,

ever stink again.

"Y-yes," stammered Hobgoblin.

"Good," said the Huntress, nudging him with her scrub brush. "Go there."

The next hour passed with Hobgoblin in a fog of terror. Horrific visions of swirling soap bubbles, purifying water, and scratchy brushes invaded his mind. His legs felt wobbly as he tromped through the chatty, twittery, very stinky forest.

Before he could see it, Hobgoblin could hear the delicate tinkle of Fresh Falls flowing into the Pool of Purity.

He and the flies gasped as they entered a slight clearing and beheld a perfectly clear waterfall. A sheet of water streamed cleanly down a sheer, smooth cliff face of polished bright blue rock. Silver twinkles of moonlight shimmered where the cascading water met the pool. It was all completely flawless—and to Hobgoblin and his flies, completely chilling.

The Huntress directed them around the slippery rocks that surrounded the Pool of Purity, right up to the gleaming waterfall.

"Go in," she said.

Trembling, Hobgoblin managed a wincing glance at the masked squirrel. The flies dashed to Hobgoblin's head and squeezed it tightly. She couldn't be serious.

"Not *into* the falls," said the Huntress. "*Behind* them."

Hobgoblin turned to the waterfall and took a cautious step on the smooth and shiny rocks. He closed his eyes tight and felt his flies quivering on his head.

The Huntress reached past him with the scrub brush and pressed an unassuming bulge in the wall of stone. At the sound of rock grinding against rock, Hobgoblin opened his eyes. He watched as a large chunk of the wall swiveled out to reveal an opening.

The Huntress pointed into the secret entrance. Hobgoblin carefully walked in and found himself in a pitch-black cavern. The sound of drips echoed across the walls and pinged in his ears.

Hobgoblin and the flies flinched at the sound of a match striking to life. Temporarily blinded, their eyes adjusted to find the Huntress staring at them, holding her torch high.

"I was sent here by Fiddlefart to give you the scrubbing of a lifetime," she said.

Hobgoblin shut his eyes tight. He slowly reached up to pet his flies one last time. Buzzing sorrowfully, the flies hugged his fingers.

The Huntress lowered the torch. "But I'm not going to do it," she said.

Hobgoblin gasped and stared directly into the squirrel's dark brown eyes. To his surprise, he saw something close to kindness.

CHAPTER 4

THE STINKY SITUATION

Hobgoblin blinked his eyes, caught his breath, and then farted loudly for several seconds. He immediately felt much better. The flies resumed buzzing nervous loops around his head.

"You're not going to scrub me?" he asked.

"No, I'm not," she said.

"But you work for Fiddlefart?"

"Yes," she said, eyes steady. "I apologize for the scare, but I had to act like I was really going to scrub you in case Fiddlefart's spies were watching.

Since no Rancidian would follow us behind Fresh Falls, it's only now that we're safe to talk."

"But you're not going to scrub me?" Hobgoblin asked again, a little confused.

"I promise I'm not going to scrub you," said the Huntress. Grimacing, she looked down at the royal badge pinned to her cloak. "Fiddlefart's cruelty and selfishness disgust me, but I've held my nose and played the role of loyal servant. I have worked hard to earn his trust."

The Huntress sat down on a wet, algae-covered rock. Hobgoblin sat down beside her.

"When I was a child, I had an experience that inspired me to devote the rest of my life to helping stinky creatures in danger," she said. "As soon as I heard that Fiddlefart had taken over Rancidia, I knew I had to help. For many years now, I have collected information, watched Fiddlefart for weaknesses, and waited for the right time to overthrow him and restore the Rancidian democracy. I believe that time is nearing, Hobgoblin."

Hobgoblin's eyes sparkled with admiration for the mysterious squirrel. From what the warthog had told him about Fiddlefart, it would take a lot of guts to stand up to someone so mean and cruel.

"What happened when you were a child?" asked Hobgoblin.

A shadow passed behind the Huntress's masked eyes.

"That doesn't matter," she said. "What matters is that you're in danger—Fiddlefart wants you scrubbed. You're the Grossest Smelling in the Land, and that threatens him. He's very self-centered. He already has all the power and wealth, now his only motivation is to be the stinkiest one of all. He'll stop at nothing to make that happen."

"I don't understand," said Hobgoblin. "The Mucklands aren't even part of Rancidia. All I do is fart around my farm and mind my own business. I've ignored this ogre stuff so the flies and I could stay out of it."

"Even though Fiddlefart is bringing the battle to you, the truth is, you've always been involved," said the Huntress. "You may not be a Rancidian, but Fiddlefart's cruelty is your business. Anytime a creature is treated unjustly—no matter who they are or where they're from—it's everyone's business."

Hobgoblin rubbed his temples. This was a lot to take in. "A warthog has told me stories of Fiddlefart.

I tried to convince myself he was making it up. Even when he stopped delivering gas, I pretended it had nothing to do with the ogre king..."

Hobgoblin trailed off. The Huntress kept her masked eyes fixed firmly on him. Hobgoblin looked away. Then, with a wince, he asked: "Is it really that bad in Rancidia?"

"Yes, Hobgoblin," she said. "Everything you've heard is true. Fiddlefart has destroyed a beautiful democracy. That reality doesn't change, even when you stick your head in the muck and ignore it. Wishing it isn't real doesn't make it go away—it just means you'll be next on his scrub list. And guess what? You're next."

"But I'm just a bean farmer," Hobgoblin

stammered. "What can I—"

The Huntress cut him off, placing a paw on his shoulder. "You have to listen to me, Hobgoblin. I have a plan that will keep you safe."

Hobgoblin straightened up. The squirrel continued.

"After the seven elected officials—the Seven Stinkers—were kicked out of the Onion Palace, I met them here in this secret cavern behind Fresh Falls. It's the last place Fiddlefart or his spies would think to look."

Wide-eyed, Hobgoblin looked around the cavern.

"Sitting here on these rocks, I helped the Seven Stinkers come up with a plan to overthrow Fiddlefart and restore the Rancidian democracy," she said. "As we wait for the right time to carry out the plan, they are hiding away, deep in the Fetid Forest. While they went away to hide, I did the opposite. I became one of Fiddlefart's minions to get as close to him as I possibly could."

As if to make absolutely certain he was accepting her words, the Huntress held Hobgoblin by the head and stared into his eyes.

"You must go to the Seven Stinkers. They and the barking spiders will protect you. Fiddlefart will eventually learn that you're still the Grossest Smelling in the Land, and he will come for you. When he does, it's better that you're with allies and not vulnerable and alone in the Mucklands."

The Huntress let go of Hobgoblin's head. "Hobgoblin, we can't force you to help us fight Fiddlefart. But, in the very least, we can keep you safe. No matter what, we won't let you become the next innocent stinky creature to get scrubbed."

She turned her dark eyes to the flies. They paused midair as the Huntress made eye contact with each of them in turn. "I know Hobgoblin isn't ready to join the rebellion, and that's OK," she said. "But I need to ask: are you, little flies, ready to step up for your fellow stinky creatures? Hobgoblin's stink—and the rebellion—desperately need your help."

She removed the sack from her shoulders and took out a glass jar.

"Fiddlefart asked me to capture the six of you as proof that I scrubbed Hobgoblin. I need you to fly into this jar so I can deliver you to Fiddlefart and fool him into thinking that I carried out his order. That will buy me time to accomplish an important task far outside of Rancidia. It will also give Hobgoblin extra time to hide out before Fiddlefart comes looking for him."

Hobgoblin was in shock. He covered his mouth and shook his head.

He wanted to protest. He wanted to grab his flies and run and never look back. He wanted to cry and shout and close his eyes and be back in his mud hut, sleeping safely with the little flies on his pillow.

Before he could say a word, the six flies had landed on the rim of the jar. Perched in a row, they saluted the Huntress.

She returned the gesture with a warm smile. The flies glided to Hobgoblin, nuzzled him on the nose, and then lowered themselves into the glass jar. The Huntress closed the lid and used a crossbow arrow to poke several holes in the top.

The flies waved to Hobgoblin from within the jar. Hobgoblin waved back, a tear sliding down his cheek. He sniffled wetly as the squirrel placed the jar in her sack.

"Now you must go, Hobgoblin," said the Huntress in a tone that was both firm and kind. "You must run as fast as you can and as far as you can into the Fetid Forest. Head northwest and don't stop until you find

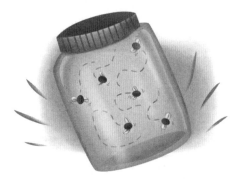

the cottage of the Seven Stinkers on the banks of the Rancid River. If you get lost, the barking spiders will find you. I have some important tasks to accomplish, and once I do, I will join you there."

Hobgoblin's mind raced. None of this was sinking in. All he could think about were his flies and his bed and his farm. He fiddled nervously with the Pre-Bean vial around his neck.

"When I blow out this torch, you must run to the safety of the Stinkers' cottage," said the Huntress. "Remember, Hobgoblin—Fiddlefart will be coming for you. Whatever you do, do not let your guard down. Your stink depends on it! Now, RUN!"

At that, the Huntress held the torch before her face and blew it out. The world went dark and Hobgoblin ran.

Hobgoblin thrashed through the forest. He left a gassy trail of green stench behind him. Moonlight shot downward in spikes here and there. But for the most part, the Fetid Forest was a dark mystery.

Branches, brambles, and barbed thorns whipped past Hobgoblin as he ran. They clawed at his arms and legs. He batted them away, but the forest only grew denser. He felt as if the plants and trees were trying to eat him alive.

He ran for hours. The Huntress's raspy voice echoed through his head, repeating in rhythm to his every step. *Now run. Now run. Now run.*

Eventually, the forest canopy opened up and moonlight streamed down in wide columns. The silver light cast an eerie shine across strange-looking plants, trees, and flowers.

Hobgoblin's nose sent distress signals to his brain. Something smelled wrong. He slowed down and sniffed the air. His eyes darted around as he tried to figure out the stench that terrorized his nostrils. It was a scent he'd never smelled before. It smelled sweet…it smelled floral…it smelled *nice*.

His heart jumped at the sight of a large patch of bright red roses. But these weren't normal roses, which would be bad enough. Maybe it was the moonlight playing tricks, maybe it was his lack of sleep. Either way, Hobgoblin watched in horror as the red roses transformed into red demon faces with hungry grins.

Dashing quickly away from the roses, he was immediately confronted by a wall of lilies of the valley. Hobgoblin shrieked. Each of the little flower bells had turned into a laughing hobgoblin skull.

Hobgoblin tried to run away from these terrifying, pleasant-smelling visions, but a group of aromatic petunias stopped him cold. He whimpered as they turned into whirring, jagged-toothed buzz saws.

He whipped around again. "Ahh!" he screamed. His only escape route was blocked by a hulking pine tree dragon. It laughed menacingly in his face. It smelled like a crisp alpine morning.

"NOOOO!" wailed Hobgoblin.

He flung his hands into the air, spun 360 degrees, and slumped dramatically onto the forest floor. Shoving his nose into the crook of his arm, he sobbed himself to sleep.

Later that night, long after Hobgoblin's sobs had become snores, another much cuter sound began to bounce off the trees: "Arf! Arf! ArfArfArf!" The high-pitched "arfs" multiplied into the dozens as they surrounded Hobgoblin's limp and helpless body.

The Fetid Forest's night sounds shifted sleepily into morning sounds. The sky glowed with a trace of yellow. And Hobgoblin's sleeping body floated along the forest floor on top of dozens of little black barking spiders.

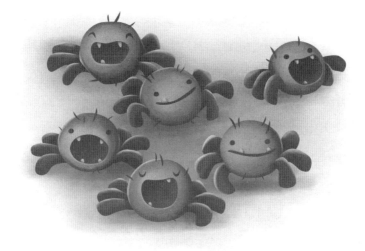

CHAPTER 5

THE BARKING SPIDERS

H obgoblin woke up beneath a quilt, his eyes crusty with dried tears. Everything was blurry. He rubbed his eyes, blinked, and—

"Gah!" He flung his head under the quilt.

Two things were certain: 1) he was in someone else's bed, and 2) he was surrounded by dozens of little fuzzy smiling faces.

He peeked out again from beneath the quilt. The little fuzzballs bounced up and down on the floor like eager puppies. Others dangled from the ceiling on thin strings of silk.

"Arf! Arf! ArfArfArf!" they barked cheerfully.

"Where am I?" asked Hobgoblin. "What are you? Some kind of bug? Some kind of spider that barks?" Hobgoblin scrunched up his brow. The trace of a memory fluttered just out of reach. Then, at once, his eyes lit up like gemstones.

"You're the barking spiders! Just like the Huntress told me about. She told me to trust you, and you seem very cute. Cute things are usually trustworthy. And, in any case, you're way less scary than those evil, nice-smelling plants. My nose has never been more offended in its entire life!"

Several spiders skittered onto the bed with Hobgoblin and cuddled in next to him. He patted them gently on their heads. A few more scampered up the bedframe behind him.

"Arf! Arf! Arf!" they barked. They each took a turn saying hello and receiving a pet.

Hobgoblin smiled lovingly at the little spiders. They reminded him of his poor, brave flies, and that made his insides ache.

He wished desperately that he and his flies hadn't gotten swept up in this ogre king stuff. He knew, though, that wishing wasn't going to get him anywhere.

With a deep breath, he turned his attention to his surroundings.

The small dirt-floored room was crammed wall to wall with seven beds. Two of the beds were doll-sized and much smaller than the others. There was a staircase at the end of the room that led downstairs.

A name was carved into the headboard of each bed. Hobgoblin read them out loud, starting with the bed he was in, and ending with the two smallest beds.

"Grody…Yucky…Icky…Musty…Fusty…Poot… and Toot."

Hobgoblin looked around at the fuzzy spiders. "Cool names. And exactly seven of them. That seems important, but I can't remember why…"

Hobgoblin shut his eyes tight, tapped his head thoughtfully, and explored every corner of his memory bank. Then, in a glorious flash, the Huntress's words from the Fresh Falls cavern waved hello from the darkness.

"The Seven Stinkers!" cried Hobgoblin, opening his eyes wide. "This is exactly where I'm supposed to be. What a relief!"

The spiders barked excitedly in response. "Arf! ArfArf! ArfArf!"

"Now, little spider friends," said Hobgoblin. "Do you know where the Seven Stinkers are? Have they gone far? Will they be back soon? Come to think of it, I don't even know *what* they are. I know they used to be elected officials, but what kind of creatures are they? Are they squirrels, like the Huntress?"

The barking spiders barked even more excitedly, bouncing up and down and gesturing wildly with their little spider arms.

Hobgoblin studied them and scratched his chin. "What is it, little guys? What are you trying to tell me?"

Several of the spiders turned to a nightstand beside one of the beds. On it lay a pickaxe and a caving helmet with a headlamp attached to it. The

spiders jumped up on the nightstand, bouncing and barking excitedly. Other spiders joined in to draw Hobgoblin's attention to the mining equipment.

Hobgoblin scratched his chin a little more and arched his eyebrows—first one, and then the other.

"Hmm," he said. "Are they cave dwellers? Perhaps bats? Maybe bears?"

The spiders shook their bodies back and forth and barked in the negative. A couple of them acted out digging, wagon pushing, and other mining activities. Hobgoblin considered them carefully.

"If I'm reading you right," he said, raising a finger, "we're dealing with a group of seven cave bears—possibly bats—who spend most of their time in a cave. They are rich bears or bats, and this is their vacation home. It's also very possible they love spaghetti and hopscotch, but I'm still piecing it all together."

The spiders made little frustrated whines and barks. As if they realized Hobgoblin wasn't going to get it, their bouncing slowed down and their enthusiasm drained away.

"Ah, well, I guess I don't understand," said Hobgoblin. "I do know that, whatever they are, they are somewhere, and they spend most of their time in that somewhere. That's clear by the unacceptable state their home is in."

Hobgoblin hopped out of the bed marked "Grody" and walked over to a much larger bed marked "Yucky." The spiders followed him along the floor, the walls, and the ceiling.

Hobgoblin wiped a finger along the top of the headboard.

"Just look at this," he said. "There's barely any dust at all."

Hobgoblin looked around and sniffed the air. He continued sniffing as he walked down the stairs and into the main room. The spiders followed.

"It doesn't even smell that bad in here," he said. "And no cobwebs anywhere. My, my, my."

In the main room, there was a little kitchen area and a long table with five chairs. On top of the table was a much smaller table with two little chairs.

An assortment of musical instruments hung on the wall across from the kitchen. Hobgoblin's eyes bulged at the sight of a tuba, but he quickly batted away the urge to play. Now was not the time for that kind of tooting.

Hobgoblin turned away from the instruments.

The barking spiders watched him with large, attentive eyes.

"These rich musician bat-bears clearly don't have time to properly stink up their home," he said. "So we're going to help them out."

Hobgoblin removed his cloak and held it in the air above his head. Two spiders swooped down from the ceiling and swung it gracefully onto a wall hook.

Hobgoblin rolled up his sleeves. He then gestured to groups of barking spiders in turn: "Now you make the cobwebs. You muddy up the ground. You mess up the kitchen. And I will fart around."

The barking spiders nodded vigorously and barked, bounced, and swung around the cottage. "Arf! ArfArfArfArf!"

Hobgoblin grabbed a few stray beans from his pocket and popped them into his mouth. He then giggled hysterically as he rolled around spreading his famous hobgoblin farts throughout the cottage. Above him, barking spiders swung from the ceiling, spreading and stretching cobwebs across every surface and within every crevice.

Together, Hobgoblin and the spiders sent gas and glee flowing through the cottage. "Don't be

shy with the tooting," suggested Hobgoblin. "A little gas really helps to set the pace!"

Several barking spiders worked together to fill pots with water from the sink, which they then dumped onto the dirt floor. Others jumped happily into the newly created mud and rolled around to spread the filth even more.

Hobgoblin farted on chairs and under the bed covers. He even farted all the way down the stair banister with one long, impressive streak of flatulence.

Barking spiders rustled in Hobgoblin's hair to cover themselves in his musky hair grease. Then, like little bees carrying putrid pollen, they spread the grease around the cottage on plates, on silverware, on candleholders and tabletops.

Drifting in from an open window, barking spiders carried in smelly green stalks of skunk cabbage and placed them in a rusty tin can at the center of the dining table.

Carried away by the joy of tooting, Hobgoblin called out: "The flies and I always sing an old hobgoblin work song when we're farming in the bean fields. Sing along with me!"

Dancing and farting across the cottage, Hobgoblin belted out:

Tooty through your duties!
Time passes fast
when you pass gas.
It helps you pass the time!

So toot a little toot!
Break in a grin
and break some wind
and you'll stay in your prime!

"ArfArf! ArfArfArf!" the spiders barked cheerfully in tune with Hobgoblin's undeniably catchy song.

They spent the entire day stinking, griming, and sullying up the cottage. Soot, grease, cobwebs, and mud now covered everything—every wall, chair, dish, floorboard, rafter, musical instrument, pickaxe, and hardhat. A smile spread across Hobgoblin's oblong face as he surveyed and sniffed their handiwork.

The gassy, action-packed day left Hobgoblin with a grumbly stomach. With the barking spiders' bouncy guidance, he found a jug of milk—extra chunky, just the way he liked it—and a brick of green bread. He settled down with his meal in a comfy chair by the cottage's front window. Outside, the Rancid River gushed noisily and stinkily at the bottom of the hill. As the sun lowered in the sky, shades of yellow coated the river's murky surface.

A barking spider cuddled into his lap and barked a happy little "Arf!"

Hobgoblin smiled. He was proud of what he and the barking spiders had accomplished, but he knew that they could have done an even better job if the flies had been there to help. And while the cottage now smelled more like his mud hut than it did before, nowhere would ever truly be home without his flies.

Holding his Pre-Bean vial in his hand, he worried about the terrifying ogre king who wanted him scrubbed. He worried about the Huntress and the Stinkers' mysterious plans of rebellion. But mostly, he worried about his flies. He closed his eyes and tried to send reassuring feelings of love across the miles that separated them.

More barking spiders snuggled in around him. They were too cuddly to resist, and Hobgoblin quickly fell asleep in the chair by the window. As soon as he drifted off, the tired, yawning spiders carried him upstairs and tucked him into Grody's bed.

The barking spiders skittered out of the cottage to enjoy late afternoon naps in their silk beds in the trees outside. They left Hobgoblin tooting peacefully in a deep sleep with visions of bean sprouts swaying serenely in his head.

Meanwhile, at the Onion Palace, the flies' experience wasn't nearly as peaceful. In fact, it was easily the most uncomfortable moment of their lives. They tried their best to remain calm as Fiddlefart waltzed with their glass jar throughout his chamber, twirling and swirling among his garbage piles.

"I smell worse than garbage! I smell like the sewer! I smell the grossest of them all!" he crooned.

This childish display had started several hours ago, the moment the Huntress delivered the flies. Fiddlefart had whipped open the door, snatched the jar out of her paws, and immediately begun whooping and fist bumping the air in celebration of his reclaimed stinky supremacy.

The Huntress didn't wait around to watch the scene unfold. She swiftly left the room and secretly saluted the flies as she closed the door. The flies found strength in her gesture, but it didn't change the fact that they were now alone and spinning through the room in the clutches of an obnoxious ogre.

Sweaty from the enthusiastic dancing, Fiddlefart clumsily slammed the glass jar down on the window sill. He snagged his grimy "Grossest Smelling in the Land" trophy and cuddled it against his clammy face.

"Oh hello, my dear," he said to the trophy. "Care to tango with me, the stinkiest dance partner in the universe?"

The ogre kissed his trophy and the flies turned away in disgust. To help drown out the ogre's off-putting conversation with his trophy, the flies wrapped their arms around each other and buzzed old hobgoblin farming songs. It made them think of Hobgoblin and it made them think of home. It made them feel as though there was a chance, however tiny, they could make it out of this alive.

As the flies continued buzzing in unison, the ogre tangoed passionately with his trophy as if the two were costars in a below-average musical.

Far below this strange scene, outside the Onion Palace, a masked squirrel made her way quietly through the streets of downtown Tooterville. Dashing past dark homes and buildings, the squirrel had the determined pace of a creature with much to do and no time to lose. Like a cinnamon-scented shadow, she slipped through the night undetected.

CHAPTER 6
THE STINKERS PASS GAS

Rings of yellow sulfide gas plumed out of Puffer Mountain in a cheerful, reliable rhythm.

While the mountaintop puffed happily, the rest of the mountain was another story entirely. Ribbons of barbed wire fence, thorny rose bushes, and warning signs snaked around the mountain's base. The signs bore Fiddlefart's royal emblem, crudely scribbled in what appeared to be red crayon.

The blockade seemed to serve its purpose—not a creature could be seen or heard or smelled for miles. It gave the once joyous mountain a sad, for-saken feeling.

But deep beneath the mountain, far from the ears, eyes, and noses of Fiddlefart's spies, a loud and stinky workday drew to a close.

At the end of a drippy and very secret cavern, a bog monster named Grody twisted several dials on a natural gas well. The short, goopy creature, who resembled a soggy gumdrop, whistled while he worked.

The well was a collection of pipes, knobs, valves, cranks, and bolts connected by a rubber tube to a metal canister on the ground.

Grody's bright yellow eyes were trained on a gauge on the canister. He watched with an eyebrow crooked, the sharp gaze of an engineer.

The gauge's needle moved steadily from the red EMPTY side to the green FULL side. The bog monster nodded and then stuck his little boggy hands into his mouth to let out a shrill whistle.

Yucky, a hulking skunk ape wearing wire-rimmed glasses, waited a little farther down the cavern. "Grody has procured sulfide! Prepare to transmit!" she bellowed. The bookish Yucky had a habit of speaking in big words that almost nobody understood.

"Grody's got gas! Get ready to pass!" translated Icky, a moss-covered sloth positioned even farther down the cavern. Icky had her own habit of rewording Yucky's vocabulary so the group would understand.

Grody the bog monster twisted the canister off of the well and passed the gas to Yucky. The skunk ape bent down and, with a cheerful grunt, hoisted the canister onto her shoulder.

She walked the canister down the cavern and passed the gas to the sloth by placing it on a flat piece of wood with wheels.

"Salutations, Icky," said the skunk ape to the sloth.

Icky smiled gently. The serene and laid-back sloth didn't seem to mind the moths, beetles, and lice that crawled about her mossy fur.

Bending down low to push the canister on the wheeled platform, Icky slowly passed the gas down the cavern. After several long moments, she arrived to the next in line: a squat mummy with sunken eyes and a snarky grin.

"Gas for you, Musty," said the sloth to the mummy.

Musty the mummy mischievously arched an eyebrow. Icky knew what was coming next: some sort of jokey comment. It seemed the only words that came out of the mummy's mouth were sarcastic or silly. Musty smirked at the sloth before addressing the pirate skeleton next to him: "Hey, Davy Bones. We got another gas can."

"AARGH!" said the pirate skeleton. He was covered in sea mold and dried seaweed and wore a pirate hat. "The name's Fusty, ya scurvy sack'a breeches!"

Musty pretended to be offended. Then he threw his bandage-wrapped head back and laughed loudly.

"Breeches," he said. "I haven't heard that word

in centuries."

Fusty the pirate skeleton didn't pay attention. He was busy fiddling with an olfactometer—a small metal box with knobs and tubes. It was an important tool for measuring the stinkiness of the gas they were mining. Of course, the stinkier the gas, the better.

Musty the mummy bent down and connected a tube from the olfactometer to the gas canister. He made sure it was tight, and then gave his friend a thumbs up.

Fusty turned a knob on the box, causing it to whir. With his black, hollow eyes he watched a gauge on the box, which had a flower on the left side marked NICE and a skull on the right side marked NASTY. The needle on the gauge moved swiftly to the skull side.

"AARGH!" said Fusty. "Th' gas be nasty today, hearties!"

Musty used a grease pencil to mark the canister with a large X, along with his initial. He then detached the canister from the olfactometer's tube. Together, the mummy and the pirate skeleton passed the gas farther down the cavern.

When they reached a large mining wagon, they lifted the canister up and placed it with a dozen other canisters, already neatly arranged. Each of them had been marked with a grease pencil X and Musty's initial.

Slapping the canister with his bony hand, Fusty called out: "AARGH! 'Nother one for ye, Toot 'n' Poot."

"Is it about time to wrap it up, guys?" Musty asked the dung beetle and dung ball sitting at the front of the wagon. "Get it? 'Wrap it up'? Because I'm a mummy…"

Ignoring Musty's joke, the beetle, Toot, chirped with satisfaction and made a mark with a little pencil on an inventory list attached to a miniature clipboard.

The dung ball, Poot, nodded. A little hand sprouted out from Poot's round body, and from the hand sprung a little thumb pointing upward.

Adopting the tune of a familiar song, Musty cupped his bandaged hands around his mouth and sang out to the bog monster at the other end of the cavern: "Hey, Gro! Hey, Gro! It's time for us to go!"

"AARGH!" called Fusty the pirate skeleton in a celebratory way.

"Indubitably, we've accomplished our quota," said Yucky the skunk ape.

"We're full of gas, Grody. Time to go," clarified Icky the sloth.

The bog monster nodded, then twisted a series of dials and cranks that whined and squealed in response. The other Stinkers waited patiently for his signal. At last satisfied that the well was shut off, Grody saluted his fellow Stinkers, and they saluted him right back.

Yucky strapped herself into a rope harness in front of the wagon, and the rest of the Stinkers climbed on board. While the skunk ape pulled the team and their gas through the cavern, Poot and Toot hummed cheerily in front. The humming progressed into singing, and before long, everyone had joined in. As large smelly drips splashed down from above, the Seven Stinkers sang their way to the cavern's opening.

And home from work they went.

Stringy clouds lined the sky and burned pink in the sunset. Yucky the skunk ape pulled the gas- and Stinker-filled wagon out of the secret under- ground mine. They passed through an opening hidden behind long, dangling strands of ivy and lichen and emerged onto a forest path.

Grody the bog monster, his brain always grinding away, silently went over plans in his head. The other Stinkers passed the time telling jokes at Fiddlefart's expense and playing classic Rancidian road trip games like Smelling Bee and I Sniff.

Eventually, they made it back to their cottage. Yucky used her impressive skunk ape strength to guide the wagon into the backyard toward a large shed. Beside the shed sat a very large and very strange contraption. It resembled a combination of an alien spaceship and some kind of futuristic washing machine.

Grody ran in front and opened the shed's swinging double doors. Yucky, Icky, Musty, Fusty, and Grody unloaded the canisters onto the shed's gas-packed shelves. Poot and Toot checked their inventory sheets to make sure everything was in order.

Once all the gas was packed away, Yucky parked the wagon on the other side of the peculiar washing machine contraption.

They made their way across the yard to the cottage, with Toot rolling Poot to lead the group. When they arrived, Toot stood on top of Poot and balanced like a circus performer as Poot rolled them up the door.

Toot grabbed the doorknob with tiny beetle hands, opened the door, and then:

BOOM!

An explosion of foul, flatulent air blew the Stinkers back across their yard and against the gas shed. It was as if the house itself had farted.

They lay in a jumbled heap on the ground, exchanging awestruck expressions.

"Flabbergasting!" said Yucky.

"Amazing!" restated Icky.

Grody helped unwedge Poot from a bramble bush. "Let's all be careful," he said. "Fiddlefart may be behind this." Having been in hiding for many years, the Stinkers grew very suspicious of anything out of the ordinary. Whenever something was out of place, it made them worry that Fiddlefart had learned about their secret plans and tracked them down.

The Stinkers cautiously made their way to the wide-open back door. Barking spiders giggled as they crowded around the windows to get a glimpse inside.

The Seven Stinkers gaped in amazement as their eyes took in the dust, cobwebs, grease, mud, and dirt that covered everything. Their noses delighted in the hair-curlingly stinky odor that had transformed their home.

"What is this? Did we get a special visit from some sort of stinky Santa Claus?" asked Musty the mummy.

Fusty wiped a bony finger along a dish, drawing a

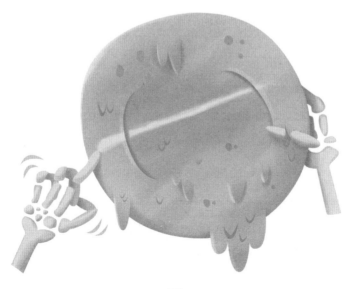

line in the grease. "AARGH! Them dishes been sullied!"

"It's never smelled worse in here," observed Grody. "How marvelous!"

Poot and Toot gave twin whistles from the top step leading to the bedroom. They chirped with excitement and waved their fellow Stinkers up to join them.

The Stinkers reached the top of the stairs and abruptly stopped.

From the bedroom came the nasally rhythmic sound of snoring...or perhaps farting...or perhaps both. It emerged from a quilted mound on top of Grody's bed.

They all listened intently. Whatever was beneath the quilt, it was snoring and tooting on alternate beats to create a hypnotic and pungent rhythm.

"That's the stinky stinker that stunk up our house!" cried Musty, pointing a mummified finger at the quilt.

The others didn't respond. They were mesmerized by the soothing pattern of snoring and farting. Grody looked around at his motionless friends. He decided to take matters into his own hands.

The bog monster jumped up on the bed and bravely yanked the covers off the sleeping stranger.

A hushed awe fell over the group as they beheld

74

the funny-looking, pointy-nosed face of a very sleepy, very confused Hobgoblin.

"You made it!" cried Grody. "And it's true what they say. You smell exactly like a fart."

The Seven Stinkers inhaled through their noses and sighed with delight. Then they greeted Hobgoblin, the Grossest Smelling in the Land, with a hearty round of applause.

CHAPTER 7

THE HUNTRESS RETURNS

A few days later, just before dusk, a winged imp landed on a tree halfway up Steamer Mountain, Puffer Mountain's sister to the south. Far above the imp, thin trails of foul-smelling vapor flowed steadily from the mountain's open top.

The light was fading as the imp unwrapped a parcel of greasy newspaper. *Ahh*. It was a fermented herring he had tricked out of a fishmonger in the Morassian market. He sniffed it dreamily.

But something else caught the imp's nose. Looking

around frantically, his eyes widened as a heavy, smelly, chestnut-colored heap of fur lumbered around the bend. The imp flapped behind the tree for protection.

The shaggy beast—a musk ox of impressive size and scent—rounded the corner. The beast carried a masked squirrel on her back and pulled a tightly tarped, fully loaded wagon behind them.

Peeking around the tree, the imp decided he'd seen and smelled enough. He made a rude gesture and fluttered away to eat his herring in peace.

As the musk ox cleared the turn, large clouds of her breath floated around in the crisp mountain air.

The Huntress patted the musk ox's thick, matted fur. "Whoa there, Moxy," she said. "Let's rest here a minute."

The Huntress hopped down. She pulled some moldy hay out of a bag strapped to the musk ox's harness. Then, feeding handfuls to her massive friend, she gazed down the mountainside to a group of glum-looking homes in a Pootonian village below.

Nearly every chimney puffed out green, yellow, and brown smoke, the result of nasty-smelling dinners busily boiling in cauldrons throughout the village. As the chimney smoke puffed lazily upward, the individual wisps blended with each other in the dusky sky above.

"Soon, Moxy, those homes will be bright, beautiful, and gassy," said the Huntress. "Just as they should be."

The squirrel's masked eyes went farther, past the Pootonian village, to the distant buildings of downtown Tooterville. Above Tooterville, the Onion Palace loomed like a weird, bewitched vegetable.

The Huntress narrowed her eyes and squeezed her punching paw. She hoped Fiddlefart didn't harm the brave flies she had delivered to his chamber. She thought of them and the many courageous creatures who made the rebellion possible. The flies, the barking spiders, the Stinkers, and her best friend of many years, Moxy the musk ox. Without Moxy's physical strength and determination, they would have never been able to travel so far in such a short time.

Over the past few days, they had journeyed deep outside of Rancidia. They had climbed over Steamer Mountain and followed the Rinsey River through the Gastric Mountains. They had trudged through every type of weather until they crossed the borderlands and arrived in a strange land where the Rinsey

River's clean and glistening waters originated. This wholesome land was bursting with daisies and rainbows and smiling faces. Everything there smelled sickeningly pleasant.

It was a difficult, uncomfortable journey, but it was also very necessary. Now, nearly back in Rancidia, they had the supplies they needed to put their plan into action.

The Huntress looked back at the tarp-covered wagon and felt a pang of disgust in her stomach. The thin tarp was all that separated her and Moxy from a stockpile of terrible, no-good, nice-smelling weapons—scented candles, potpourri, incense, bathroom spray, and the like.

Blech! she thought, making a throw-up face.

To find this wicked collection, she had acted on a tip from a cyclops witch who was passing through Rancidia. The witch directed her to that strange, happy land where a young, lovely smelling, and very pale woman lived with seven little men in a perky cottage.

The Huntress found the woman to be nice enough, even if she smelled like flowers and sunshine.

The nice woman expressed sympathy for

Rancidia's troubles and happily agreed to donate these hideous weapons of mass fragrance. Her assistance came despite the protests of one of the little men, who seemed to have a bit of an anger problem.

Before leaving, the Huntress offered her deep thanks. She solemnly swore to somehow repay the pale lady's favor one day.

The Huntress petted Moxy and smiled. The musk ox responded with a grumble of pleasure.

They had to move on. The entirety of Rancidia was at stake, and there was still so much to do. The weight of the revolution was on the Huntress's shoulders, but she was OK with that. She had been risking her life to protect stinky creatures for almost as long as she could remember. It wasn't even a choice. It was simply what she had to do.

The Huntress climbed onto Moxy's back and gave a spirited whistle. The musk ox grunted affectionately, and they were off. The wagon swayed side to side as they made their way down the mountain.

It would be a couple days before they reached the cottage of the Seven Stinkers. And before they could reunite with their fellow rebels, they had one more stop to make along the way: the dreaded, sanitary waters of the Pool of Purity.

Meanwhile, high above downtown Tooterville, the six flies watched from their jar as three stinkbirds worked up the courage to try, once again, to land on their favorite Onion Palace window ledge. At the precise moment the birds' smelly little feet touched down, anger thundered out from within the chamber.

"She lied to me!? These flies are lies!?"

The stinkbirds flapped away in startled disarray. It was time to find a new favorite window.

Inside the chamber, Hobgoblin's flies glared defiantly at the ogre king from within their jar on the window sill. The Burping Bullfrog repeated himself:

> *As long as Hobgoblin lives*
> *you just can't compete;*
> *Compared to his funky scent,*
> *you smell almost sweet.*

The ogre stomped childishly across the chamber,

slapping at stacks of garbage. The flies followed his every movement. Despite the circumstances, they did feel a small twinge of pleasure watching Fiddlefart make the whirlwind transition from happy dancing to tantrum throwing.

"She was my most loyal minion," he whined. "She did everything I asked, swiftly and without question. She even smelled like cinnamon!"

Fiddlefart pulled a rotten apple from a heap of garbage and squished it in his colossal hand. "Cinnamon!" he yelled again, for some reason.

The ogre shook his head, as if to erase unpleasant thoughts.

"Fine, whatever," he said, pretending to be over it. "There's a reason I'm the king instead of someone else. I'm the only one I can trust, so I might as well take matters into my own hands."

He positioned himself in front of the bullfrog. "Now, tell me, Frog: Where is he?"

Head up the Rancid River
to the forest's brink;
You'll find Hobgoblin hiding
in a house of stink.

"Excellent," said the ogre, glancing over to the flies. The flies stared back, unblinking. "But first, I must deal with these six-legged liars."

Fiddlefart snatched the jar up from the window sill and dangled it outside.

Their little fly hearts pounded as they gawked at the buildings of downtown Tooterville far below.

Suddenly, the ogre whipped the jar back inside the chamber.

"Nah," he said. "That would be too easy. I have something more painful in mind."

He casually tossed the jar to the bullfrog. The frog caught it with his moist, squishy hands.

"Here," said the ogre king. "Have a snack."

The bullfrog licked his lips. His mouth oozed saliva. Waddling backward, he disappeared with the flies into his hole in the wall.

CHAPTER 8

THE REEKY RECITAL

With his green aura of stench wafting around him, Hobgoblin sat in a chair at the Stinkers' long and dirty dining table. Before him was a nearly finished bowl of frothy fungus stew. As he did during every quiet moment, Hobgoblin rolled the Pre-Bean vial in his fingers and thought of his flies. Several barking spiders were curled up asleep in his lap.

The Stinkers, who weren't bat-bears after all, had recently returned home from their workday in the mine. They were now scattered throughout the cottage, relaxing and settling in for a pleasant evening.

Over the last several days, Hobgoblin had fallen into a nice domestic rhythm with his seven hosts. Every day, when the Stinkers headed to work, he stayed back at the cottage to fart around with the barking spiders.

Finishing the last bite of his fungus stew, a satisfied Hobgoblin leaned back in his chair and looked around the room.

In the far corner, by the wall of instruments, Yucky the skunk ape and Icky the sloth admired a patch of marvelously layered cobwebs. Hobgoblin watched a moth flutter out of the sloth's green-stained fur, and then dart back in for safety at the sight of barking spiders dangling from the ceiling.

Grody the bog monster sat across the table. He was hunched over engineering plans of some kind, a pencil stuck into the gelatinous side of his head (where Hobgoblin assumed his ear might be).

At the other end of the table, Musty the mummy and Fusty the pirate skeleton were engaged in a heated game of Stinkopoly. It was heated, mostly it seemed, because Fusty didn't know the rules.

Meanwhile, Toot the dung beetle was balancing on Poot the dung ball like a practiced acrobat. Poot barreled them swiftly across the floor, stopping at each of the candle sconces lining the room. Poot rolled up the wall beneath each sconce so that Toot could light every candle with a match. They continued rolling and lighting until the entire cottage glowed with warm candlelight.

Hobgoblin admired these Seven Stinkers very much and appreciated their friendliness. But, despite their kindness and the stinky comforts of their cottage, he found it difficult to relax and enjoy himself. Everything was dragged down by the sadness of missing his flies and by his longing for the return of his simple, comfortable life in the Mucklands.

Hobgoblin looked out the window at the Rancid River whooshing past at the bottom of the hillside.

Grody hopped onto the table, walked across, and placed a swampy hand on Hobgoblin's forearm.

"Don't worry, buddy," said Grody. "The Huntress will return soon, and then we can carry out our plan to defeat the ogre. Once he's out of the picture, we'll reclaim our democracy and reunite with our families—including you and your flies. Just have a little faith."

Hobgoblin tried to smile, but it was more like an awkward grimace.

From the end of the table, Musty offered, "I've been a mummy for thousands of years—if I can be optimistic about this, I think you can too. Don't sweat it. We'll see our families again soon."

"AARGH!" said Fusty. "Miss me sea cap'n pappy."

A barking spider woke from his nap and yawned lazily on Hobgoblin's arm. Hobgoblin petted the spider softly on the head while Grody spoke.

"It's been many years since Fiddlefart kicked us out of the Onion Palace," he said. He reached into a drawer beneath the tabletop and pulled out a gavel. He held it up high, like a sword. "We've been forced to trade the council room for the gas mines, but our goal remains the same—to do what's right for Rancidia. Right now, the best thing we can do for our country is get rid of the ogre king. We spend every day mining sulfide gas not just because we love the work, but because it's an important part of our plan to kick Fiddlefart out of Rancidia once and for all."

Grody tapped the gavel against the engineering

plans on the table. "Plus, it helps us look ahead to a brighter, stinkier future. Once Fiddlefart is ousted, Rancidians will need gas to power their homes."

Hobgoblin smiled as he pictured himself with his flies back in his mud hut, sulfide gas pumping strong. He imagined the yellow gas powering his mud hut's light fixtures and flowing through the vents. It was bright, toasty, and oh so stinky. He was halfway through a sentimental sigh when a tooting sound blared through the cottage.

Hobgoblin looked up to see Yucky the skunk ape adjusting the mouthpiece on a contrabassoon, while Icky the sloth warmed up a trombone. The

Stinkers weren't only former council members and current gas miners—they were musicians to boot.

"Boisterous jamboree, commence!" cried Yucky.

"It's party time!" reworded Icky.

The Stinkers and barking spiders whooped with glee.

In a clanging bustle, Musty, Fusty, Poot, and Toot pulled instruments off the wall. The spiders in Hobgoblin's arms darted onto the table and along the wall to get a good view of the upcoming performance.

Never ones to miss a party, more barking spiders crawled in from outside.

"I think we know what will cheer you up," said Grody. He grabbed the tuba off the wall and handed it to Hobgoblin. "We noticed you eyeballing this earlier."

Hobgoblin's tub-shaped face lit with glee, and immediately his worries scurried away. They were no match for this shiny brass distraction.

"Set the rhythm, Fart Man!" called Musty as he adjusted the grip on his trumpet.

"AARGH!" cried Fusty. He propped an empty jug on his knee bone.

Poot and Toot readied their kazoos as the Stinkers

formed a circle.

Hobgoblin began tooting a rhythm—"Prumpf, prumpf, prumpf, prumpf, prumpf..."—and the Stinkers joined in with their instruments.

The barking spiders barked and howled in tempo with the music.

When the symphony of toots was off and running, Grody jumped into the middle of the musical throng and began to sing.

> *Far away from here,*
> *live my neat-freak relatives.*
> *Sure, they're nice and all,*
> *but some things you can't forgive!*

He somersaulted over to the skunk ape and gestured toward her with both boggy hands. The tooting skunk ape returned the gesture with a wink.

> *Yucky uses big words,*
> *far too huge to understand.*
> *Or, as she might say:*
> *They're "grandiloquently grand!"*

Grody skipped over to the tromboning Icky and pointed to a little beetle crawling along the sloth's arm.

Bugs and lice reside
in her fur from end to end.
Where she goes she brings
a universe of friends!

Grody danced his way to Musty and smiled as the trumpeting mummy eyed him with exaggerated fear.

Forgive Musty's snark,
he's just grinding up your gears.
You'd be sassy too
if you'd been a corpse for years!

Fusty, on the other hand, was too focused on blowing on his musical jug to notice Grody's verse one way or another:

Fusty is unhinged,
but it keeps us on our toes.
When he talks we nod,
but what he means, no one knows!

Grody cartwheeled over to Toot, who was balancing on top of Poot, both of them kazooing like mad. Then, after sharing a glance, the dung beetle and dung ball dropped their kazoos. Poot split himself into three equal parts, and Toot juggled the three little Poots with gusto. Grody sang:

Two peas in a pod,
they stick together like glue.
But that's not so hard
when your friendship's full of poo!

Throughout the rowdy recital, barking spiders bounced around on the window sills, tables, and floor with adorable, squeaky fits of laughter. Each Stinker had to take occasional breaks from tooting when overcome by giggle fits.

Inspired by Grody's performance, Hobgoblin decided he would give it a try. Handing his tuba to the bog monster, he jumped into the circle. Grody kept the deep tuba toots flowing as Hobgoblin riffed:

> *Eat beans, tooty toot!*
> *Tooty toot, a magic fruit!*
> *Toot tooty and tooty toot!*
> *It's a hoot to tooty toot!*

Everyone in the room buckled over in laughter at Hobgoblin's crude but spirited performance.

As they tried to collect themselves and keep the hoedown alive, a trio of outgoing barking spiders hopped into the middle of the group. Bouncing up and down to the faltering rhythm, they sang:

> *Arf, Arf! Arfy Arf!*
> *ArfArfArfArf! ArfArf! Arf!*
> *Arfy! Arf, Arfy!*
> *ArfyArfyArf! ArfArf!*

Hobgoblin, the Stinkers, and the barking spiders collapsed on the ground, rolling around with joy. Hobgoblin wiped laughter-tears from his eyes as he looked around the room at the diverse creatures all sharing a blissful moment together.

Although he felt very far from the comfort of his flies and the bean farm, Hobgoblin was beginning to understand the value of a larger community. He was starting to see why the Stinkers and the Huntress were so committed to bringing back Rancidia as it once was. Each of these Stinkers represented a unique district, they each came from a completely different background, and they each blessed the world with their own particular stench. And yet, here they were, living, laughing, and tooting as equals.

Tears of laughter blurred his vision, so he may have been mistaken, but when Hobgoblin looked around the room, what he saw looked very much like a family.

CHAPTER 9

THE MADDEST COW

King Fiddlefart sat alone, stewing with jealousy. He had just sentenced Hobgoblin's flies to death by frog, but it didn't make him feel any better.

"What is a hobgoblin anyway?" he muttered to himself. "I know what a goblin is, but what's a 'hob'? It doesn't make sense."

Looking at his bookshelf, the ogre declared, to nobody in particular, "He deserves much more than a scrubbing. I'm going to get rid of him once and for all. The world will be better off without him and his hob stinking it up."

Fiddlefart stood up and pawed the spines on the top shelf of his moldy bookshelf. He passed titles like *The Fart of War*, *Land Conquering for Dummies*, and *Think Stinky Be Stinky* before ripping down a leather-bound volume. He slammed it onto the table in a way that no reasonable creature would treat a book.

He flipped to the title page—*Various Creatures and How to Murder Them*, by N. Chantress—and grunted with approval.

"Let's see," he said, flicking to the index in the

back of the book. He scanned the H section with one of his infected index fingers. "Harpy... headless horseman... hellhound... hippogriff... Ah! Here it is: hobgoblin. Page 352."

Eagerly hunched over his book, Fiddlefart could easily have been confused with a monstrous middle school student cramming for a test.

The ogre found his way to the hobgoblin entry and studied it intently.

CREATURE: *Hobgoblin*

SCIENTIFIC NAME: *Smelticus Delticus*

PERSONALITY: *Kind, Naïve, Gullible, Easily distracted, Loyal*

FAVORITE FOODS: *Beans, Stinky cheeses, Turd blossoms*

ALLERGIES: *Soap (causes sleeping death)*

MURDER SUGGESTION: *Hobgoblins are gullible and easily distracted. This fact, combined with their love of stinky cheese and their serious allergy to soap, leads the*

*author to recommend magically disguising
a cake of soap as a wedge of stinky cheese.
(Follow the easy-to-use recipe on the next
page.) Once one makes the enchanted
soap, one must make eye contact with the
hobgoblin while slowly cutting the cheese.
Without question, the hobgoblin will accept
the gift, eat it, and then fall into a sleeping
death.*

MURDER-SPELL REVERSAL: *Under special
circumstances, the spell may be reversed by
a rare and powerful Heritage Fart.*

"A Heritage Fart?" Fiddlefart read out loud. "How peculiar." He scratched the putrid warts on his chin.

Fiddlefart flipped to the next page to view the cheese-soap recipe. Then, like the monster he is, he ripped it right out of the book.

Holding the recipe close to his face, he felt a shudder ripple through his body. "Soap. *Gross!*" he said. "The things I do for self-esteem."

Fiddlefart stomped over to his walk-in closet and tore through the piles of stinky, sweat-stained clothes that made up his wardrobe.

He sifted past a werewolf mask, a police uniform, vests and cloaks made of exotic fungi and molds, sparkly boots, and a dairy cow costume. The cow outfit gave him an idea. Petting the fake cow pelt, he purred, "Not yet, my darling. Not quite yet…"

At last, Fiddlefart lumbered out of the closet wearing the outfit he'd been looking for: a hazmat suit that covered him in protective yellow plastic from head to toe. He wasn't going to take any chances working with something as loathsome as soap.

Like a yellow space alien not quite used to the planet's gravity, he walked stiffly down the spiral staircase to the royal pantry. When he arrived, he stood before the Royal Pantry Keeper: a baggy-eyed hedgehog sitting behind the pantry's front desk, slumped over a crossword puzzle.

The hedgehog looked up, screeched in horror, and jumped out of his seat. "Invasion!" he screamed.

"Scram, Pokey," said the ogre, with a "get outta here" thumb gesture.

The hedgehog, whose name was most certainly not "Pokey," hopped over the counter and scrambled into the stairwell. He left his crossword puzzle behind, vulnerable and unfinished on top of the desk.

Like an ogre in a china shop, the hazmat-suited king lumbered clumsily through the pantry. He knocked over shelves, swiped items onto the floor, and generally caused a big mess. The hedgehog not named Pokey would have been horrified. Fiddlefart was cruelly destroying weeks of careful work that went into organizing the royal pantry's massive stockpile.

Alas, thanks to the hedgehog's organization, it didn't take long for Fiddlefart to load up a rusty bucket with the recipe's ingredients: lye, extra-virgin lizard oil, owl pellets, mouse pellets, Chupacabra scale, cheese culture, kraken ink, lichen rennet, hemlock root beer, essence of demon, water, twine, and a little frog's breath to disguise the smell.

Hauling the loaded bucket in both hands, he shuffled slowly back up the staircase. Along the way, he passed the poor hedgehog cowering in a corner.

Back in his chamber, Fiddlefart pushed a pile of garbage and moldy food off a table and lifted a cauldron into the cleared space. He emptied the bucketful of ingredients beside the cauldron and cracked his chunky knuckles.

Whipping his head back and forth between the recipe, the pile of ingredients, and the cauldron, Fiddlefart tossed in items, stirred, squeezed, whispered magic words, mashed, zested, and crushed. The cauldron poofed, fogged, screamed, boiled, and shivered with each new step.

Eventually, with his forehead dripping large globs of sweat, Fiddlefart pulled from the cauldron a steaming wheel of cheese at the end of a long piece of twine.

Holding the cheese cautiously at arm's length, the ogre stared with bloodshot eyes at his creation in excited, nervous wonder.

Then, as if seamlessly on cue, lightning struck outside the chamber window. In the split-second blaze of light, the cheese revealed its true nature: a cake of soap. When the lightning flash disappeared, it became cheese once again.

Fiddlefart's triumphant cackle shook the walls, windows, and garbage piles of his chamber. Now that the soap was safely transformed into cheese, he felt comfortable removing the hazmat suit and slipping into his disguise of choice: the dairy cow costume.

Staring at his reflection in a grubby full-length

mirror, the ogre admired himself for an uncomfortable amount of time.

"Not bad, Fiddlekins," he muttered, raising a flirtatious eyebrow. "Not bad at all."

With one last wink to the mirror, Fiddlefart exited through the back of the castle into the morning fog. He tromped down to the banks of the Rancid River and hopped into someone's creaky fishing boat.

The raving king paddled noisily against the current, toward the Fetid Forest. From darkened homes, sleepy creatures peered through their window shutters and gasped. There appeared to be an insane cow mooing with glee and giggling his way up the river.

CHAPTER 10
A CHEESY DOWNFALL

Morning sunlight streamed into the Stinkers' cottage. It cast a golden shimmer across their stinky pre-work bustle. Hobgoblin sipped on snail-trail tea as the seven friends got ready for another day in the gas mine.

Icky the sloth, wearing a cave helmet with a headlamp, dangled from a light fixture that was no longer in use. Beneath Icky, Yucky strapped on her size 29 boots.

As they always did before they left for the secret gas mine, the Stinkers asked Hobgoblin if he remembered the most important rule. But, every day, it was as if he was hearing it for the first time. Memory was not Hobgoblin's strong suit.

"Have you memorized our consultations, good fellow?" asked Yucky, not looking up from her boots.

"Remember what we said, Hobgoblin?" restated the upside-down Icky.

Hobgoblin looked up from his tea, his face as blank as new fallen snow. "Yes," he said. "Make sure to water the skunk cabbage before sundown."

"Nope, that's not it," said Musty, who was fastening a strap on the overalls covering his mummy bandages. "No disrespect, pal, but sometimes I wonder if your brain is made of farts."

Hobgoblin narrowed his eyes in concentration.

"Umm..." he said, stalling. "...don't wake up Fusty if he's sleepwalking because then he'll never wake up?"

"AARGH!" replied Fusty, slipping needle-nose pliers into the belt hanging on his moldy hip bones. "'Tis a sad but true tale, matey."

"Nope, not that thing either," said Musty. "It's the *other* other thing."

Hobgoblin tapped his head, thinking hard.

"...Always be true to myself?" he ventured with a hopeful smile.

Grody, who was going over some plans with Poot and Toot, jumped up on the table and held Hobgoblin's head between his spongy bog monster hands.

"All of those things are true," he said. "But there's one specific thing we need you to remember when we're at work today. Can you remember what that one thing is?"

Without moving a muscle, Hobgoblin stared into

Grody's glowing yellow eyes. Then, matter-of-factly, he said: "Never look a gift horse in the mouth."

"NO!" the Stinkers yelled in unison. The barking spiders chimed in with squeaky exasperation. "DON'T TALK TO STRANGERS!"

Grody wiped a hand across his face, composing himself. "Look, Hobgoblin, I know this is hard for you to remember, but it's very important. I'll start from the beginning: It's safer for you to stay here while we're in the mine. It's too risky for you to leave the cottage—you could easily be spotted by one of Fiddlefart's minions. But, when he finds out that you're unscrubbed and stinkier than ever, he might come here to find you. He may disguise himself, so your best bet is to simply *avoid talking to strangers*."

"Ah, darnit," said Hobgoblin, shaking his head. "Now I remember. Don't talk to strangers."

"AARGH!" said Fusty. "Wicked wiles!"

Grody surveyed the Stinkers. They all patiently waited for him to give the green light. "Alright, team. Let's move on out. We've got a whole lotta gas to pass."

The Stinkers lined up, and each in turn gave Hobgoblin a high-five as they left the cottage. Poot and Toot brought up the rear. When they reached Hobgoblin, they bounced in the air, side by side, to deliver a high-five to both of Hobgoblin's hands at once. The two chirped their goodbyes, and Hobgoblin closed the door.

As soon as it clicked shut, Hobgoblin let out a long, multi-pitched fart. It was a particularly funny one, and it made him laugh. As he turned away from the door, he brought a finger to his lip and said, "Wait, what was I supposed to remember?"

Barking spiders threw their legs in the air with little whines of woe.

Hobgoblin farted around the cottage, doing his best to keep it stinky for the Stinkers. A feeling nipped and nagged at him. He was supposed to remember something, but the something escaped him. The harder he worked to chase it down, the further it burrowed into the depths of his mind.

"Wicked wiles..." he guessed. "...or was it something to do with sleepwalking? Or was it the gift horse thing? What is a gift horse, anyway?"

A loud BANG! BANG! BANG! from the door interrupted his twisty train of thought. He welcomed the interruption. Trying to remember things was hard work.

The barking spiders were far less welcoming—they growled loudly. It was cute and menacing at the same time.

"Oh, shh," said Hobgoblin to the spiders. "This might be the gift horse himself."

Hobgoblin flung open the door to reveal a large, strange-looking cow standing on two hooves and holding a wheel of cheese on a piece of twine. The cheese looked—and smelled—absolutely delicious. Gray, nasty-smelling gases swayed in the air around it. It was completely enchanting.

Hobgoblin's mouth watered as his nose sniffed hungrily. The cow watched with an evil grin, his plastic udders fluttering in the wind.

"Maybe it was a gift *cow*, not a gift *horse*," said Hobgoblin, eyes locked on the cheese.

"Moo! Moo!" said the cow. "I'm here to offer you a free sample of my world famous stinky cheese. It's the stinkiest, most repellent cheese ever made. You'll love it!"

"ARF!ARF!ARF!ARF!" Barking spiders hopped up and down around Hobgoblin, barking emphatically. The cow tried to kick at one of them with a fabric hoof.

Hobgoblin blinked his beady eyes. "Well, you don't seem to be sleepwalking. I've already watered the skunk cabbage, and if I'm being true to myself, I have to admit that I love cheese, so...come on in!"

Growling and snarling with fury, barking spiders swooped down from the roof and into the cow's face. Some sprayed silk into the cow's eyes, while others scrambled up his legs and tried biting through the fabric of his cow suit. None of it worked—he was just too big. He brushed them away and entered the cottage.

"I'm sorry, Gift Cow," said Hobgoblin. "The barking spiders are usually much friendlier."

"Ah, never mind them," said the cow with a sneer. "I'm sure His Grotesqueness, King Fiddlefart, will soon scrub the land of disrespectful pests."

"Hmm, I don't know about that," said Hobgoblin. "I try to stay out of politics, but Fiddlefart seems like a bad guy to me. Musty calls him a flower sniffer."

"Silence!" roared the cow, before clearing his throat and looking about the room sheepishly. "Haha, I mean, moo moo! Let's eat some cheese."

The cow set the cheese on the table and pulled out a kitchen knife from inside his cow suit. Then, making eye contact with Hobgoblin, he slowly cut the cheese.

A scrumptious aroma of garbage, rotting meat, rancid mold, and, strangely, a hint of frog's breath danced in Hobgoblin's nose.

Completely mesmerized, he reached for the cheese wedge.

The barking spiders erupted in desperate panic. They dive-bombed Hobgoblin from the rafters and crawled up his legs and torso in a sprint to reach the cheese before his mouth did.

But Hobgoblin didn't notice. He was too distracted by the delicious cheese.

He took a bite. The barking spiders screeched in terror.

Instantly, the glorious flavors of decay and mold disappeared. Hobgoblin gasped as his mouth was invaded by the taste of 10,000 spring wildflowers blossoming in a hidden meadow. It was a sparkling clean, soapy taste that reminded Hobgoblin of nothing so much as death.

He gagged and sputtered. He twirled around the

room in the throes of the soap-cheese's toxins. Then, suddenly, the Stinkers' warning returned to his mind.

"Oh, now I remember," he said, and collapsed to the floor. "Don't talk to strangers."

Evil belly laughter rolled through the cottage. "Who's a flower sniffer now!?" roared the cow, triumphantly.

Barking spiders swarmed the cow from the floor and the ceiling. Their attack only made him laugh harder as he slapped them away and stumbled out of the cottage. He cackled all the way to the wobbly fishing boat on the riverbank, hopped in, and paddled away.

Back in the cottage, barking spiders crowded around their fallen friend. Like a funeral of tiny wolves, they pierced the air with mournful howls.

CHAPTER 11
A FART FOR THE AGES

From within his hole-in-the-wall bungalow, the Burping Bullfrog awoke from a restless slumber. Removing one of his earplugs, he sighed with a smile.

At last, the earsplitting clatter of Fiddlefart's clanging, poofing, grunting, and deranged laughter had gone quiet. The Burping Bullfrog could finally bask in the calm silence of the ogre's absence.

He glanced at the jar of flies. The little critters were still staring at him. As far as he could tell, they hadn't taken a break from giving him the evil eye since he brought them into the chamber. Their bold-ness creeped him out a little.

No matter. Courageous flies taste the same as weak-willed flies: crunchy on the outside, squishy in the middle, and delicious all the way through.

Stomach gurgling, the Burping Bullfrog waddled over to the glass jar. He tried to avoid the flies' eye contact, but he failed. Their defiance seemed to have a magnetic force all its own. It drew the frog's eyes to them against his will.

The Burping Bullfrog blinked. "Get it together, frog," he thought to himself. "These are flies, and you're a bullfrog. This is all perfectly natural."

The bullfrog sat with the glass jar between his legs. He began to twist the lid open with his slimy hands. Then a melodic buzzing sound made him stop.

With their arms around each other, the flies buzzed a tune that the Burping Bullfrog immedi-ately recognized.

"Tooty Through Your Duties," he whispered, astonished.

All at once, the bungalow vanished, and the Burping Bullfrog was transported back several centuries to his tadpole years in the

Unincorporated Mucklands.

Life was easy back
then. He spent his days
splashing around in the
muddy muck, listening
to the hobgoblin family
farming in their bean fields
and singing their work songs.

They were always very nice to him. They offered
him bean dishes every morning and every night. He
was so full of beans, it wasn't until much later in life
that he developed a taste for flies.

Everything changed when he grew from a tadpole
into a frog and discovered his magical all-smelling
powers. When others found out about his mys-
tical sniffing abilities, he was whisked out of the
Mucklands. The last few hundred years had been
a blur, ping-ponging around at the command of
various nobles, queens, kings, and other creatures
of power in and outside of Rancidia.

The bullfrog had grown accustomed to this life,
but it was a far cry from his humble beginnings in
the Mucklands. Back then, the hobgoblins were nice
to him because he shared their land. Not because

they wanted to use him to become powerful or gain wealth. They were nice because they were neighbors. And back then, that's what neighbors did.

The Burping Bullfrog looked at the flies, who continued to buzz their song as they stared right back at him.

His stomach growling, the bullfrog rolled his bulbous eyes with irritation.

"Fine," he said. "I won't eat you."

Finally breaking their ice-cold stare down, the flies looked at each other in disbelief as the bullfrog opened the jar. They zoomed cheerfully into the air and saluted the bullfrog.

The Burping Bullfrog opened his bungalow door and turned to the flies. He sniffed the air deeply. With eyes closed, he intoned:

Consider this, little flies,
then fly away fast:
To save Hobgoblin's future,
tap into his past.

The flies exchanged puzzled looks. With the Burping Bullfrog's words echoing in their minds, they zipped from the bungalow, through Fiddlefart's chamber of garbage, out the open window, and into the cold night.

Remarkably, all it took was a quick sniff of the nighttime air for the flies to pick up on Hobgoblin's scent. Along with Hobgoblin's odor came the distressing, unmistakable whiff of soap. With a gasp, they bolted away in pursuit of their best friend.

The Burping Bullfrog, whose stomach was very angry with him, put on a pot of lily pad stew. While he waited for the stew to warm up, he closed his eyes and transported himself back to when he was just a small tadpole in the Mucklands with his entire life ahead of him.

With both paws, the Huntress held on to Moxy's tangled fur. The musk ox leaned into the weight of the jam-packed wagon as they made their way through the lush and stinky Fetid Forest. After their stop at the Pool of Purity, the wagon was even heavier now. But the extra weight didn't slow Moxy down—this, at last, was the home stretch. In just a few more miles, they'd reach the Stinkers' cottage.

Even though she was so close to her destination and surrounded by the forest's familiar aromas and sounds, the Huntress's stomach ached with worry. For the past several hours, she battled the feeling that no matter how fast they went, they would be too late to save Hobgoblin.

She tried to shake the feeling. She tried to take comfort in the thought that their efforts were much bigger than the life of one hobgoblin, or squirrel, or fly. But it didn't help.

As if she shared the Huntress's feelings, Moxy moaned dismally into the night air.

"I know, girl," said the Huntress. "Let's hurry."

The wagonload creaked as Moxy picked up the pace. The Huntress felt a renewed urgency to get to the Stinkers' cottage, if only to confirm with her eyes what her heart already knew.

In the light-tinged darkness just before dawn, the Huntress and Moxy lumbered up the hill of the Stinkers' front yard. The Huntress swiftly unhitched Moxy from the wagon, gave her a quick pat, and ran to the cottage. Moxy gave her friend an encouraging groan and then, with a grunt, slumped down in the grass outside the cottage door.

Inside, the Huntress found the Stinkers standing around Hobgoblin's body, their heads bowed dismally. The poor bean farmer lay on the dining table with stalks of skunk cabbage in his clasped hands. He was snoring loudly, with little soap bubbles drifting upward from his mouth, popping without a sound against the ceiling.

Barking spiders nestled around Hobgoblin, some of them sleeping restlessly, others howling and whimpering in dismay.

The Huntress stayed near the entrance and choked back emotions as she took in the scene. Around the table, the Stinkers sobbed and muttered.

"Poor guy just couldn't remember our warning," said Grody. "We should never have left him alone." A tear trailed down his goopy body and plopped on the dirt floor.

Yucky was so sad, her usually advanced vocabulary escaped her. "Such a bummer," she said. She removed her glasses and wiped stinky tears from her furry cheeks.

"Such a bummer," said Icky. "Wait, what?" Momentarily confused, she looked up at Yucky. She shook her head and then quickly resumed mourning her friend.

"I'll get the ceremonial mummy bandages ready," said Musty, his typical sarcasm at rest for the moment. "We don't usually wrap a non-Cryptonian with traditional mummy bandages, but we'll make an exception for Fart Man."

"AAARGH!" said Fusty sadly. "Th' hearty shall git a proper sea burial 'neath Methanian waters!"

Musty glared at Fusty in offended disagreement. Poot and Toot jumped up on the table and chirped softly into Hobgoblin's ear.

With a deep breath, the Huntress walked through the room and placed a hand on Grody's head. Grody looked up at her, tears framing his yellow bog monster eyes.

"It looks like a sleeping death," he said. "We came home from the gas mine and found him on the floor. Beside him we found a wedge of soap with a bite taken out. Fiddlefart must have enchanted it somehow."

"We must be strong," said the Huntress, her head bowed. "We have to stick to our plan and free

Rancidia in Hobgoblin's honor. His loss will not be forgotten."

"Indubitably despicable," whispered Yucky the skunk ape, regaining her words.

"Just isn't right," said Icky the sloth with a sigh.

The sound of frantic buzzing entered the cottage. Everyone turned to see six flies rocket in through the window. The flies halted in midair at the sight of their friend lying on the table.

With anguished cries, they plunged down to Hobgoblin. Poot, Toot, and the barking spiders cleared space so the flies could hug Hobgoblin's snoring face.

"I'm so sorry, brave flies," said the Huntress. "Hobgoblin would have been so proud of you for escaping Fiddlefart's chambers. His legacy, and the legacy of the hobgoblins, will live on in you."

"AAARGH!" said Fusty, squeezing his pirate hat to his rib cage. "Th' last o' the 'goblins!"

"It's so sad," said Grody, watching the flies sob miserably atop Hobgoblin's head. "After so many centuries of hobgoblin farts stinking up the Mucklands, the world has smelled its last."

The flies perked up at Grody's words. With the

abruptness of a light turning on, the Burping Bullfrog's mysterious advice suddenly clicked in their minds.

Together, the flies made a piercing squeal that sounded not unlike the word "Aha!"

The flies wiped their tears and then buzzed frantically around Hobgoblin's neck. They pulled his Pre-Bean necklace into the air and dropped it on his chest. They pointed at the vial, squeaking as if their little fly heads were on fire.

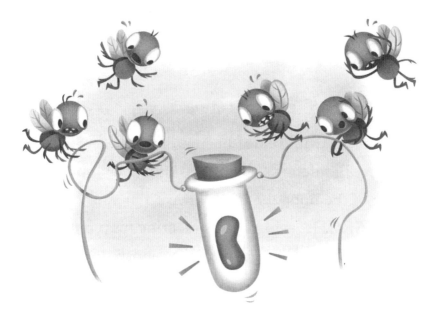

"Hmm," said Yucky. "They implore us to eradicate the legume."

"They want us to get rid of the bean," reworded Icky.

The flies cried out in negative, agonized chirps. They pointed excitedly at Hobgoblin's open mouth.

"ARGH!" suggested Fusty. "'Tis a cursed bean!"

"Nah," said Musty. "I think they want to keep the bean as a memento."

The flies dropped down on the table in defeated exasperation.

"I think," said the Huntress, walking up to the table, "they want us to feed the bean to Hobgoblin."

The flies nodded and whizzed around the room in happy loops.

The Huntress carefully uncorked the vial and dropped the bean into her paw. Every breath in the room was still. Every heart beat like a hummingbird's (except for Fusty, who didn't have a heart).

The Huntress slowly, gently placed the bean inside Hobgoblin's wide open mouth.

The room watched, completely silent.

Then Hobgoblin's intestines gurgled, and everyone jolted back.

There was another gurgle, another moment of silence, and then:

BUH-BOOM!

From Hobgoblin exploded a fart so intense that it shook his family tree to its roots. It was a real-life Heritage Fart—a fart so powerful that every one of Hobgoblin's ancestors felt it, no matter where they were in time, space, or dimension.

The fart was so powerful, it blew Grandma Hortense's and Grandpa Horace's hair back. They were enjoying a game of pinochle in hobgoblin heaven—the Great Stink Cloud in the Sky. It sent their cards fluttering right off the table.

The fart was so powerful, it whooshed back in time to rock Great-Aunt Fartunia's muck bath, sloshing her and the muck right up and out of the tub.

The fart was so powerful, it thundered all the way back to deliver a gloriously stinky blast of wind into the face of Stenchingham Hobgoblin at the very moment he planted the first hobgoblin bean seed in the Unincorporated Mucklands.

The fart was so powerful, it blasted the Huntress, the Stinkers, the barking spiders, and the flies across the room and against the wall. It also awoke Hobgoblin from his sleeping death.

Bolting upright with a gasp, Hobgoblin stared

quizzically at his friends. They lay tangled and astonished on the floor.

"Hey, uh…" he said, holding his head. "It smells great in here. What happened?"

Blinking their eyes, everyone in the room looked at Hobgoblin in disbelief. The most wonderfully wretched scent they had ever smelled occupied their noses, wafted through the room, and continued to grow in power and potency. They had all just experienced the fart of a lifetime, and, indeed, of Hobgoblin's actual life.

CHAPTER 12

THE REBELLION SWELLS

Everyone was overjoyed at Hobgoblin's stinky comeback, but nobody was happier than the flies. They looped in delighted circles and embraced Hobgoblin's smelly head. They missed every part of him, but mostly it felt good to buzz around in his one-of-a-kind stench once again.

"I'm so happy you're safe!" said Hobgoblin with happy tears in his eyes. "I still can't believe how brave you are. You're the best flies a hobgoblin could ask for."

Hobgoblin's wide smile slowly dissolved into a confused frown. "But, wait," he said. "When did you get back? Why am I on this table?" He put a hand on his stomach as his intestines trembled with gurgly Heritage Fart aftershocks.

Musty the mummy patted Hobgoblin on the shoulder. "Biting into soap was a terrible decision," he said. "But I'm glad you're alive, pal."

"AAARGH!" said Fusty. "Th' 'goblin's back!"

Hobgoblin rubbed his head.

Grody eased Hobgoblin's head back down on the table. "Take it easy, Hobgoblin," he said. "You've been through a lot lately."

The Huntress pulled up a chair beside Hobgoblin. She placed a comforting paw on his arm. "I know it's difficult, but can you remember anything after the Stinkers left for the mines?"

Hobgoblin squinted his little eyes. He stared up at the ceiling, straining to remember.

"There was a cow…with stinky cheese," he trailed off with a shudder. "…I bit into the cheese, and when I woke up, everyone was on the floor."

"Astounding flatulence, comrade," said Yucky, sniffing the air with her mighty skunk ape nostrils.

"Best fart ever," rephrased Icky, whose critters nodded in agreement from within her moss-saturated fur.

Poot and Toot nodded in wide-eyed admiration.

"We can assume the cow was Fiddlefart," said the Huntress. "I've walked in on him wearing a cow costume before."

The Huntress cringed and shook her head. "We're just glad you're alive, Hobgoblin," she said. "Soon, we'll make sure that tyrant doesn't hurt any stinky creature ever again."

The Huntress raised a paw. Everyone, including the spiders and the flies, gave her their full attention.

"Listen up, Stinkers," she said. "In no time at all, Fiddlefart will learn that Hobgoblin survived. Once he does, he'll come back here to finish the job. You all know the plan, and everyone knows their role. We just have some final steps to make sure everything is ready to go."

"The plan seems good and all," said Musty with a mummified smirk. "But wouldn't it be easier if we just chase the ogre onto the edge of a cliff and hope that lightning strikes at the right moment to send him tumbling down?"

The Huntress rolled her eyes. "I think you've been watching too many movies, Musty."

Musty's jokes aside, the Stinkers and the Huntress discussed the details of their plan. Hobgoblin's brain was still quite foggy from his recent experience. But, despite the fog, something was starting to come into focus.

"Excuse, me," said Hobgoblin at a pause in the conversation.

"Yes, Hobgoblin?" said the Huntress.

Still lying down, staring up at the cobwebbed ceiling, Hobgoblin continued. "We hobgoblins have always kept to ourselves in the Mucklands with our beans, our flies, and our farts."

Hobgoblin propped himself up on his elbow and

looked around the room at the kind, diverse faces. He settled his eyes on the Huntress.

"You all have taught me a lot over these past few days. You've taught me that life is better when you have a community. It's a special feeling to get out there and mingle your stink with your neighbors.'"

The Huntress and the Stinkers smiled at Hobgoblin.

"So, I guess what I'm trying to say," he continued, "is that I'm ready to chip in and help save Rancidia."

The Stinkers and barking spiders shouted with glee. Poot and Toot danced in circles on the floor with their hands in the air. The resistance had gained its newest, and stinkiest, member.

"We're honored, Hobgoblin!" said Grody.

"Superlative!" said Yucky.

"Great!" said Icky.

"Welcome to the team, Fart Man," said Musty.

"AAARGH!" said Fusty. "Th' 'goblin's aboard!"

"That's wonderful to hear, Hobgoblin," said the Huntress. "You'll know what to do when the time is right. Just trust your instincts. For now, you should rest."

A flurry of activity electrified the cottage. Everyone

darted around, completing the final touches in preparation for an ogre-sized showdown.

Hobgoblin lay back down on the table. The flies nestled into his hair, and barking spiders cuddled around him on the table. Everything, for the moment, was as it should be. The bean farmer beamed up at the ceiling. Not only was he alive, but his life felt richer than ever.

A tremble rattled through the Burping Bullfrog's bungalow. He opened one eye, then the other. When the bungalow shook again, he tentatively removed an earplug.

From the other side of the wall, he heard:

Burping Bullfrog in the wall,
who smells grossest of them all?

The bullfrog groaned as he lowered himself from his bed.

A fist banged against the wall, followed by: "Hurry hurry hurry! Hobgoblin's gone! My supremacy is restored!"

The bullfrog opened his door and shuffled out onto the little platform in the chamber wall.

Over the years, he had seen Fiddlefart under a variety of strange circumstances. But nothing had prepared him for this. The ogre king stood there in a dripping wet cow costume clutching a paddle, a monstrous smile stretching from ear to ear.

Fiddlefart's crazed and happy eyes were covered in twisty red veins. It appeared as if the ogre had traveled through the night without so much as a single potty break.

The Burping Bullfrog cleared his throat. "Um, right. Here goes then."

This time, the bullfrog's eyes didn't roll back in his head, he didn't inhale the air around him, and he didn't tremble, rumble, or even belch. Instead, he took a deep breath. Then, in a straightforward tone, he said:

> *I can smell across the world*
> *close in and abroad,*
> *but it doesn't take magic*
> *to know you're a fraud.*

Fiddlefart's jaw dropped like a broken drawbridge. Stunned at this display of disrespect, he didn't move a monstrous muscle for several long seconds.

The Burping Bullfrog took advantage of this pause to wrap up his thoughts on the matter:

Hobgoblin is still alive,
you silly nitwit.
Oh, and if you couldn't tell:
adios, I quit.

Before Fiddlefart had a chance to smack him with the paddle, the Burping Bullfrog darted back into his bungalow. He slammed the little door and locked the deadbolt.

Climbing up on his bed, the bullfrog closed his eyes and smiled. While Fiddlefart's furious tantrum gathered steam on the other side of the wall, the Burping Bullfrog calmly inserted the earplugs back into his ears.

CHAPTER 13

THE AWFUL STINK EYE

F iddlefart had experienced some very bad moods during his generally grumpy life. This was by far the worst.

Still in his cow outfit, which grew filthier by the minute, the ogre paddled with fury up the Rancid River toward the Stinkers' cottage. Even with the current working against him, the ogre's anger propelled him so fast, he might as well have had a motor.

The morning dawn brought lightness and twinkly

cheer to the river and surrounding land. Fiddlefart was having none of it. He tried to calm down using his smell-empowerment mantra. But every time he tried, it just turned into hateful mutterings.

"...*I smell worse than garbage, I smell like the sewer, I smell...revenge! I'll squash you, Hobgoblin! And you, too, squirrel! I'll squash you, Hobgoblin!...*"

The crazed ogre slashed at the water as if it had wronged him. As he furiously made his way up the river into the Fetid Forest, creatures scurried down into burrows and up into trees at the sound of his noisy approach.

With spittle flying, he screamed to anyone who could hear: "You'll all pay for this! Mandatory baths! Deodorant for all! I'll make sure I'm the only one who stinks!"

After many hours of this personal struggle, the ogre at last slammed the fishing boat into the shoreline near the Stinkers' home.

He glanced up the hill to the path leading to the cottage. Everything shined with the happy light of morning.

It took him a few seconds to notice it. And when he did, a plume of angry mucus rocketed out of his nose. There was sulfide gas—*illegal* sulfide gas—pumping out of the brightly lit cottage at the top of the hill. It surrounded the merry home like a pungent morning fog.

Somehow, even with this criminal gas usage, Fiddlefart had not reached the limits of his anger. But he got much closer to his limit when Hobgoblin appeared on the cottage porch with a friendly wave. The ogre nearly passed out with rage.

Hobgoblin gave a cheerful "follow me" gesture and took off up the path toward Puffer Mountain.

Fiddlefart ripped off his cow outfit and flung it to the ground. He screamed a primal, confused, bellyaching scream. It sounded like a million babies had their binkies taken all at once.

The ogre trudged up the hill in pursuit of Hobgoblin.

No more spells, no more disguises, no more smoke and mirrors. Fiddlefart was going to take care of this once and for all. He would simply pick Hobgoblin up and toss him over the cliff. Problem solved.

Stomping up the hill, Fiddlefart imagined Hobgoblin pathetically flapping his arms as he plummeted down. Just as his mental image of Hobgoblin hit the ground, the real Hobgoblin took a turn and disappeared behind a tree.

Fiddlefart ran to the tree and stopped—three figures had stepped out from behind it to block his path.

The ogre gaped. Even though they wore bandanas on their faces and clothespins on their noses, he recognized three former council members that he had kicked out of the Onion Palace many years ago: the bog monster from Morassia, the skunk ape from Fungalo, and the sloth from Lousyana. He gaped even harder when he noticed they all were armed with burning scented candles and cans of bathroom spray.

"Greetings, Your Phoniness," said Grody. He pushed down on his bathroom spray to send a puff of sugar cookie scent into the morning air. Fiddlefart recoiled with a whimper.

"Salutations, oppressor," said Yucky. She waved a large scented candle around to create a swirl of pumpkin spice scent.

"Hi, bully," said Icky. She unleashed a puff of orange vanilla bathroom spray. As terror ripped through his body, Fiddlefart swore he could see little creatures in the sloth's fur, yelling at him and gesturing angrily.

Fiddlefart covered his nose and took off up the steepening path away from the cottage. Consumed with panic, he had momentarily forgotten Hobgoblin. Escaping from this nice-smelling attack was all that mattered now.

Like the most freshly scented mob ever assembled, the trio marched slowly and steadily after the ogre.

Fiddlefart wheezed as he gained elevation up the mountain path. Then his wheeze turned into a sputtering screech—the hill had flattened to reveal a wall of smoke blocking his path.

Out from the smoky haze stepped two more former council members: the Cryptonian mummy and the Methanian pirate skeleton. They were both coolly twirling metallic balls that released fragrant incense smoke in fat, billowy puffs. They also wore bandanas and clothespins.

"We're here to knock some scents into you," said Musty.

"AAARGH!" said Fusty. "Let's smoke tha scurvy mackerel!"

Fiddlefart squealed in terror and covered his face

with his gargantuan hands.

The mummy and the skeleton casually twirled their incense balls. The billowing smoke was too much, forcing the ogre to stumble-sprint farther up the path away from the cottage.

Fiddlefart swiped at his face in an attempt to stop the sweet-smelling smoke from invading his nostrils and his eyes. It didn't work. He lost control of his lumbering feet and spilled face first onto the ground. Pawing at his eyes, he sat up on his knees.

At the sound of buzzing overhead, he looked up and whispered, "Oh no."

Six flies soared toward him like a jet squadron. They each carried what appeared to be a net made out of spider silk. In each net rested a multi-color bath bomb.

In colorful succession, the bath bombs rained down to form a semi-circle around their target. The terrified ogre shrieked in dismay and desperately tried to plug his nose with his fingers. Barking spiders scurried up and splashed cups of water on the bombs, causing a foamy, lovely smelling, and rainbow-colored blockade to blossom around the ogre king.

Fiddlefart was trapped. In front of him he had a fizzy barrier of prettily fragranced bath-bomb suds and a frightening throng armed with clean-smelling terror. Behind him was the steep, jagged cliffside. He wasn't sure which was worse—crashing to his death on the rocks below, or getting scrubbed by this aromatic arsenal.

Before Fiddlefart had a chance to choose, the Stinkers cleared a space in front of him. He watched, helplessly, as the remaining two former council members—the dung ball from Pootonia and the dung beetle from Tooterville—hurtled toward him. Toot was swiftly rolling Poot and closing in on the ogre. Without losing speed, Toot flipped over Poot and used the momentum to catapult Poot in the air toward Fiddlefart's face.

Fiddlefart swiped in panic at the approaching dung ball. He missed. With a big smile, Poot hovered for a split second in front of Fiddlefart, held up a perfume bottle, and then puffed a puff of honeysuckle fragrance right in his nose.

The ogre wailed in agony, and the rebels roared in celebration. The ogre spat and snorted and cursed.

Fiddlefart's cursing was stopped short by an assertive whistle. He looked up to see the Huntress and Hobgoblin staring calmly back at him. The Stinkers took a step back to give them room.

The ogre's panicked fear immediately turned into anger. Bursts of steam whisked away from his giant head.

"You," he hissed, pointing to the Huntress. "You betrayed me."

"No," said the Huntress. "You betrayed Rancidia and stinky creatures everywhere."

"Ha," scoffed the ogre. "You're not stinky. You're just a dumb squirrel who smells like cinnamon."

At that, the Huntress ripped off her cinnamon cloak, shook off a fake squirrel tail made of musk ox fur, and flung away her wooden mask.

A gorgeous black and white skunk stood proudly before them all.

The Stinkers and Hobgoblin looked at each other in astonishment. They had all heard folktales of the marvelous creature known as a skunk, but everyone in Rancidia assumed the stories were make-believe. The idea of a skunk—a creature that could spray a horrendously stinky spritz from its backside—seemed like it was out of a fairy tale. And yet, here she was, as real and wonderful as anything.

"My name is Niffy," said the skunk, puffing out her magnificently striped tail. "My family and I were driven out of our home country for being stinky. Not all of us made it out alive. From that moment forward, I have devoted my life to saving stinky creatures from cruel monsters like you."

The ogre king gawked. It looked as though someone had removed his brain and replaced it with a dollop of curdled yogurt.

Hobgoblin took a deep breath and stepped toward Fiddlefart. "The Huntress and the Stinkers have

taught me a lot about being a good neighbor and a good friend. I'm done farting around."

Hobgoblin's eyes flared with determination.

"From now on," he said. "I fart with purpose."

Hobgoblin and Niffy turned around to face the Seven Stinkers. With their backs to Fiddlefart, they bent their knees, pointed their butts toward the ogre, and smiled.

Fiddlefart snapped out of his stupor. They had their backs to him—now was the time to make his move. Adrenaline pumping, he decided to charge these two rebels and end this silliness once and for all. With an anguished roar, the ogre plowed through the bath bomb suds with his enormous hands outstretched.

Hobgoblin squeezed his eyes tight, and Niffy lifted her tail high into the air.

His face contorted in disgust and fury, Fiddlefart charged forward through the rainbow foam and into the close personal space of the skunk and the hobgoblin. But then—

"Hey, ogre," said Hobgoblin. "Take a whiff of this."

With Hobgoblin farting and the skunk spraying, the duo delivered a stinky explosion so forceful, so unbelievably foul, that the ogre king flew backward right off the cliff. The pungent blast was so potent that Fiddlefart's right eye clamped shut forever and his mouth froze into a permanent grimace.

This was the first stink eye in recorded history. And to this day, it is still the most awful.

Grody adjusted a pair of goggles and slipped on rubber gloves. He gave his friends a salute and scrambled down the cliffside after the ogre, hopping from rock to rock.

The falling, flailing ogre didn't hit the ground— instead, he splashed inside the Stinkers' specially made washing machine contraption waiting below. It was filled with magic, cleansing water from the Pool of Purity. It was connected to a large canister of sulfide gas.

Grody jumped down and slammed the top of the contraption shut.

He locked it tight, opened the sulfide gas valve to power the machine, and pressed the ON button. Fiddlefart splashed, banged, and shouted within.

The gas-powered machine clanked and whirred into action. Inside, a fury of brushes and scrubs, shampoos and soaps mixed with the sanitizing, deodorizing Pool of Purity waters to give Fiddlefart a scrubbing so powerful, so intimately thorough, that the ogre wondered if he'd ever smell like anything other than soap again.

Grody gave everyone a thumbs up from below. The group hollered, hopped, hugged, and high-fived above.

The machine sloshed the ogre around in the purifying, soapy waters. It scrubbed his every last millimeter, and then scrubbed some more. When, at last, the machine had run through its cycles, the lid popped open and a blast of rosy fragrance surged up into the sky.

CHAPTER 14

THE STENCH OF FREEDOM

Wide-eyed and hushed, everyone watched as the ogre sluggishly crawled out of the washing machine contraption. Not a fly buzzed, not a spider barked. Nobody so much as blinked.

When the ogre emerged from the machine, everyone gasped. He had lush, curly hair, the luminous skin of a face-soap model, and a permanently floral aroma to go along with his awful stink eye. Every inch of him twinkled like a disco ball in the sunlight.

As the ogre stood there in a soap-shocked daze, the group relaxed. The cleanse seemed to go deeper than just the surface. There was no trace of menace. It was as if his anger had been scrubbed clean away, as if his brain had been washed along with everything else.

Several seconds stretched into what felt like years. Then, shielding his permanently stink-eyed face from the sun, Fiddlefart gazed up the cliff. He gave the group a quiet wave, slowly turned around, and stumbled off to the southeast toward Steamer Mountain. He disappeared into the lush forest and was never seen, or smelled, again. (Rumor had it that he eventually followed the Rinsey River out of Rancidia and started a new, nice-smelling life somewhere near the friendly lady who lived with the seven little men.)

Everyone watched, holding their breath and their farts. The precise moment the ogre was no longer visible, the stinky saviors shifted from perfect silence to full-blast carnival. At last, the national nightmare was over. With hoots and toots, they made their merry way back to the Stinkers' cottage. They didn't walk back so much as float, riding high on a wave of stinky freedom.

When they arrived, they immediately began planning a victory parade that would take them zigzagging across the seven districts of Rancidia all the way to the Onion Palace. They would pass gas and good news to everyone they met. They would recover the Onion Palace and reclaim their government in the name of democracy. Tomorrow, they would embark at the first light of morning. Right now, however, was for partying.

For the rest of the day, the heroes let loose by tooting horns, breaking wind, sharing stories, and making up songs. They guzzled jugs of fizzy sludge, gulped down fuzzy bread, and passed around plates of stinky cheese (the unenchanted variety). After the sun went down, the party continued far into the night beneath the magical glow of fairy lights in the Stinkers' backyard.

Musical toots bopped through the night air. A fog of sulfide gas pumped across the yard, covering everything in a heavenly, stinky haze. Barking spiders swooped down through the gas clouds from the trees above. The flies surfed the muggy currents of air blasting out of every horn.

Toot juggled three Poots while balancing on Fusty's tooting jug. Some Stinkers tooted their horns, while others took turns blowing into the olfactometer and giggling at the results.

Niffy the skunk leaned against a rotten apple tree, tapping her foot in time to the rowdy music. She laughed as Musty shimmied past, tooting his trumpet with sassy abandon.

Niffy felt a nudge on her arm. She turned to find Hobgoblin holding two mugs of fizzy sludge. Accepting one of the mugs, the skunk clinked hers against Hobgoblin's and said "Thanks!"

"Actually, I wanted to thank you, Huntress," said Hobgoblin. "Oh, oops. I mean, Niffy."

Niffy smiled and took a sip of sludge. "That's 'squirrel lady' to you, buddy."

Hobgoblin laughed. "I can't believe I called you that."

"There's no need to thank me, Hobgoblin," said Niffy. "I'm just doing what's right."

"Well that's the thing," he said. "You've taught me so much about what's right over the past few days. I've learned a lot about myself and my place in the community."

Gathering his thoughts, Hobgoblin took a long gulp from his mug. "I know that eventually you'll probably leave Rancidia to go save other stinky creatures," he continued. "And I know I'm not the bravest or the smartest one around…but I want you to know that I'm ready to pitch in."

Niffy smiled and gave Hobgoblin a warm hug.

"If you could ever use the help of a clumsy bean farmer and his six brave flies," said Hobgoblin, "we're ready to support any stinky creature who's treated unjustly—no matter who they are or where they're from. Just like you helped us."

The flies swooped down to give Niffy's head a

tight squeeze. In the background, the Stinkers roared with delight as Fusty banged on a steel drum with his detached femur bones. Until that moment, nobody even knew he could do that. It was fascinating.

"Thank you, Hobgoblin. Thank you, flies. I'll check in with you next season," said Niffy. She sounded tough as ever, but Hobgoblin could detect a slight tinge of emotion.

"We would love that," said Hobgoblin while his flies nodded enthusiastically.

"It was an honor fighting the stinky fight with you," she said.

"We'll always be here for you," said Hobgoblin. "I can't trust my brain all the time, but I can always trust my nose. And this smells like the beginning of a beautiful friendship."

THE EIGHTH DISTRICT OF RANCIDIA

G rody went over their victory parade route using the light attached to his mining hardhat. It was just before dawn. Stinkers and spiders were strewn about the cottage on the floor, in their beds upstairs, on window sills, and across table-tops. Hobgoblin snored and tooted rhythmically from the chair by the front window. Niffy was outside, chatting quietly with Moxy in the dewy morning grass.

Consulting Poot and Toot, Grody made a few last-minute adjustments to the route. He set his pencil down with a pleased sigh—he was certain they had charted the most efficient course to reach each of the seven districts on their way to the Onion Palace.

With the plans set, Grody winked at Poot and Toot and picked up Musty's trumpet from the table. Poot and Toot readied their kazoos. The trio then marched and tooted loudly throughout the cottage to wake everyone from their short-lived slumber. The few groans of protest quickly transitioned into excitement—today was the day of the historic victory parade! Everyone wiped the sleep from their eyes and got to work.

They packed the wagons with stinky snacks, musical instruments, and as much sulfide gas as they could safely hold. Niffy tied the wagons together and harnessed Moxy to the front. Despite the hulking load, the musk ox pulled the wagons with merry ease.

The journey would take many days, so even among the wild merriment, the Stinkers would have plenty of time to brainstorm and discuss plans for their first council meeting when they made it back to the Onion Palace.

Before getting there, they journeyed through each district so every Stinker could reunite with their family, friends, and hometown citizens. The group, who would come to be known in history books as Rancidia's Rebels, delivered news of Fiddlefart's scrubbing, tooted merrily, and passed gas to all. The parade grew in size at each new stop, as Rancidians of all stinks, shapes, and sizes joined the jubilant procession.

The first stop was Yucky's district: the humid, scholarly forests of Fungalo, where the words were enormous and the libraries overflowing. In anticipation of the robust vocabulary of Fungaloans, Icky unzipped a backpack stuffed with pocket dictionaries and quickly passed them out to the group. While they weren't able to look up every word Yucky and the Fungaloans used, everyone clearly understood the joy and excitement they communicated.

Next, they visited the sluggish jungles of Lousyana, where Icky greeted a variety of relaxed Lousyanan citizens. In moldy treehouses at the top of Lousyana's massive canopy of trees, Icky reunited with her calm family of sloths. This family reunion took a while, not only because sloths aren't the swiftest creatures, but also due to the many little beasties in every sloth's fur. Icky waited patiently as her community of lice, moths, beetles, and assorted bugs reunited with her family's critter communities in turn.

Then they arrived at the foamy pecan-colored waters of Methania, a mostly underwater district. Fusty sprinted—quite fast for a skeleton—and jumped off a barnacled dock into the water. He floated down and out of sight with arms spread wide like a crab. No one knew what it was like down there in those murky depths, and, frankly, they didn't care to find out. After several hours greeting his fellow citizens beneath the waves, Fusty emerged riding the head of a whale skeleton. His father, a moldy sea captain skeleton with a beard made of kelp leaves, sat behind him. The sea captain greeted the group with a hearty "YEEEAARRGH!"

In the soggy bogs of Morassia, Grody's fellow citizens couldn't have been prouder of his engineering heroics. Morassians value math and science more than anything, so everyone crowded Grody to get a good look at the washing machine blueprints that were so crucial to freeing Rancidia. Nobody,

however, was prouder than Grody's two moms. They hugged Grody so hard, the three of them seemed for a moment to merge into a single three-headed bog monster.

The group visited Musty's family, friends, and dusty citizens in the parched deserts of Cryptonia. When they made it to Musty's neighborhood, his family emerged from sandy catacombs and mausoleums. Just like Musty, his family's way of showing love was through good-natured teasing. Along with lots of hugs, Musty's relatives asked him sarcastic questions, like, "Gee, what took so long?" and "Wait, it's been a while—who are you again?"

In the gaseous dirt mounds of Pootonia, Poot was greeted as a hero by every Pootonian they met, including his mother. Also a dung ball, Poot's mom looked so similar to her son that none of the Stinkers could distinguish them. Only after Poot and Toot performed their juggling trick did the Stinkers figure out how to tell them apart—Poot's mom was the one with a disturbed look on her face.

The confetti rained down as the victory caravan made its way through the crowded urban streets of Tooterville. Yucky held Toot up high so that all the Tooterville citizens could catch a glimpse of their heroic elected official. The parade ended at a Tooterville junkyard, where Toot's aunt had been living beneath a broken refrigerator. She was ecstatic to be reunited not only with her nephew, but also with Poot's mom, her dear childhood friend. Everyone cheered as Toot's aunt gleefully rolled Poot's mom in festive laps around the junkyard.

When they arrived at the Onion Palace, the crowd shuffled cheerily into the grand and stately council room on the palace's first floor. The Stinkers, representing the districts and diversity of their beloved country, sat in their rightful places around the circular and stately council table. Everyone else sat down within the many rows of seats facing the Stinkers.

Grody took his place in the middle of the round council table, with his fellow Stinkers in chairs wrapping around either side. The bog monster pulled out his gavel. "Welcome back, buddy," he whispered to it. Then, smiling at the joyful faces in the crowd, he banged the gavel assertively on the table. "I now call to order the re-assembled Elected Council of the Seven Districts. Rancidia is a democracy once again!"

A happy roar of shouting, applause, farts, and spider barks exploded from the crowd and echoed loudly off the council room's walls. Grody allowed the commotion to continue for several minutes before banging the gavel again to resume the historic council meeting.

In quick succession, the Stinkers made a series of announcements before the packed council room. They officially re-legalized sulfide gas. They named Niffy a Rancidian Knight in Stinking Armor. They bestowed Hobgoblin, Moxy, the flies, and the barking spiders with Rancidian Medals of Stinking Bravery. They even presented the Burping Bullfrog with a Certificate of Stinking Commendation for sparing the flies' lives.

Then Grody banged his gavel and said, "Brave Hobgoblin and brave flies, please approach the council table."

Unsure what was going on, Hobgoblin walked up the council room's steps, stood before the Stinkers, and took a deep bow. The flies stood at attention on Hobgoblin's head, saluting proudly.

"The Elected Council recognizes your crucial role in the freeing of Rancidia," said Grody. "We also recognize the role you and your ancestors have played in keeping Rancidia stinky for many centuries. Even if the Unincorporated Mucklands are not technically a part of Rancidia, hobgoblins have kept us all happy, full of beans, and gassy for a very long time."

Hobgoblin blushed. His flies nodded proudly.

"On behalf of the Elected Council of the Seven Districts," said Grody. "We hereby invite the Unincorporated Mucklands to become the Eighth District of Rancidia!"

The flies squeaked in delight, and the crowd cheered from the seats. Hobgoblin held his head in shock.

The Seven Stinkers stood up, walked around the council table, and approached Hobgoblin. Musty presented the bean farmer with a shiny badge with

the number 8 emblazoned on the front. "What do you say, Fart Man?" asked Musty, slapping Hobgoblin on the back.

Hobgoblin looked at his flies, who nodded vigorously in return.

"We would be honored to join Rancidia," he said. An explosion of cheers, barks, and celebratory farts coursed through the room.

Grody banged his gavel to make it official, and the Stinkers closed in on Hobgoblin with a heartfelt and foul-smelling group hug. With that, Rancidia grew a little bigger, a little muckier, and a whole lot stinkier. The seven districts became eight forevermore.

Dizzy with emotion, Hobgoblin looked into the crowd to find Niffy. There she was in the seats, beaming proudly back at him. Hobgoblin sat down on the steps of the council room. The flies dived, dipped, and swirled above his head. His heart brimmed with feeling. As if to make room for these swelling emotions, Hobgoblin let out a loud, sustained, and glorious fart.

It was Hobgoblin's first fart as a democratic citizen. It was, without a doubt, the happiest fart of his life.

ACKNOWLEDGMENTS

My deepest thanks to Andrea Reuter and Jenny Bowman for their formidable editorial insight and guidance; to Reneé Yama and the lovely people at Hazy Dell Press for their collaborative spirit and invaluable contributions; to Derek for his typically unstinky illustrations and ground-level collaboration; to Ellie for her patience and support; and to Astrid, for all the wake-up calls and morning chats.

Don't miss the full range of Hazy Dell Press books
by Kyle Sullivan and Derek Sullivan:

Chapter books (ages 8-12)

Look for *Hazy Fables Book #2*, the follow-up

to *Hobgoblin and the Seven Stinkers of Rancidia*,

coming Fall 2020.

Picture book (ages 5-12)

The Cyclops Witch and the Heebie-Jeebies

Board books (ages 1-7)

Monster ABC

Goodnight Krampus

Get Dressed, Sasquatch!

Hush Now, Banshee!

Don't Eat Me, Chupacabra! / ¡No Me Comas, Chupacabra!

All books available at **hazydellpress.com**,

and in stores everywhere.